I0518248

Dr. Grigsby's Clients

Just Jewel

ISBN-10: 0-9910521-3-7

ISBN-13: 978-0-9910521-3-4

Library of Congress Control Number: 2019909010

Book cover design by Germancreative

Printed in the United States of America

Thank you to anyone who has ever asked when the next book is coming. Thank you to my beta readers. Thank you to anyone who reads this.

1 CHRISTOPHER

"Please don't shoot," the bank teller begged with her arms raised as she cowered. The area below her arms instantly became drenched with sweat. Two circles seeped through her chiffon blouse, changing the ocean blue fabric to navy.

"Don't move and I won't have to." Christopher instructed calmly, yet sternly, with his gun aimed at her temple. He hopped over the counter and made his way to the open vault. One of his accomplices moved swiftly, clearing out all of the cash drawers in the front. It was insane that in this day and age, the year 2015, the branch hadn't invested in a bullet proof window to separate the tellers, and the money, from the patrons. One look, and it was obvious that the bank had been long-standing. Another henchman stood guard by the door to the only entrance, and a third walked around with his shotgun leading the way, bullet in chamber. His job was to make sure nobody moved a muscle in this small branch. If anyone tried to play hero, he'd been instructed by Christopher to shoot without hesitation.

Christopher was the mastermind and ring leader behind this five-man operation. The fifth member, Julio, sat outside in the getaway car. *This is getting too easy*, Christopher thought as he cleared out the vault. This was the eleventh bank the crew had knocked over within five months, and the police still had no idea who they were. Christopher, an NYU dropout, went through great lengths of strategic planning to foster the perfect robberies. He studied the blue prints of each bank and spent months in advance casing each branch, learning the full roster of employees and their work schedules, in and out, including breaks. He knew the days and times the armored trucks came and went. Having been in and out of prison a few times for petty charges, he made all the right friends. In doing so, he learned what each cash drawer of the banks contained, down to the exact count of each bill. One of his former fellow inmates even schooled him on how to identify which bills were marked or which had dye packs. He had the number and location of each panic button memorized. If he sensed a teller was even thinking of reaching for it, he kept his finger on the trigger. He also timed the traffic patterns of their escape route, cross referencing Google maps with physical maps that he was able to acquire at a local AAA. Julio was made to go through several dry runs before Christopher felt comfortable with his timing. Nothing was left to chance.

Barely twenty-one, Christopher held an intelligence far superior than that of his peers. Accepted into Yale, Princeton, and Stanford after high school, ultimately, he decided to attend New York University on a partial scholarship. With a mother who was one of New York City's highest regarded oncologists and a father who was a savvy investor of all things oil, Christopher viewed his parents as the epitome of success. With an IQ of 142, he found life at NYU to be mundane and unchallenging, opting to drop out of the university after only the first semester.

Aside from brains, Christopher was very easy on the eyes. Standing at 5'8, he'd begun to fill out nicely once he left his teen years behind. He took pride in his appearance, hitting the gym every day – sometimes twice a day; evident in the way his T-shirts hugged his torso and arms just right. Despite his androgynous exterior, the tribal band tattoo that ran around his bicep seemed to tip the ladies off that there was a bad boy hidden somewhere beneath. Something about his short, brown, curly hair screamed *I'm soft. Come touch me!* His green eyes complimented his olive complexion nicely.

With his looks and level of intelligence, Christopher could've easily charmed his way into a regular job of some sort. The excitement, the adrenaline, the guns, the skill, however, is what appealed to him more. When a bank job was done, and the team had gotten away scot-free, there was a different type of satisfaction obtained knowing it was pulled off under his leadership. It was proving to be an unquenchable craving as he turned this into his full-time career with no intention to quit any time soon.

"One minute!" Mack, the gunman guarding the door, called out. Whimpers and low muttering could be heard from the bank patrons that lay with their bellies pressed against the worn, maroon, carpet.

Christopher reemerged from behind the steel door of the vault and hopped back over the counter with two laundry bags in one hand, each partially filled with cash, and a semi-automatic pistol in the other. "Line 'em up and fall out, fellas!" He instructed.

One by one, the crew filed into a single line in their respective positions. Lemmuel, the one with the shotgun who they referred to as "Lem", would be last to leave, backing out behind the crew to keep an eye on everyone until they were safely back on the street. As he stood in the doorway, inching out steadily, but quickly, he noticed movement out the corner of his eye. It was the rope that hung between two stanchions, swinging back and forth. Just beneath the rope, lay the bank guard who moved to reach for his weapon. BOOM! Lem beat him to it, blowing a hole in his shoulder. The guard managed to let off one shot, shattering the glass pane just left of the door, before falling limp on the floor in agony. Deep dark blood spurted onto the carpet. A woman lying on the floor next to him, holding her son close to her chest, began to scream as she shielded the boy from the horror.

"Oh shit! MOVE! GO! GO! GO!" Lem yelled, before turning and running at top speed to the waiting getaway car. The four of them piled into the green 2001 Nissan Maxima, Christopher in the passenger seat. Lem didn't even have the door shut before Julio peeled off from the curb, cutting off a yellow cab as he did. In minutes they were back on the New York Thruway headed back to the city.

"What the hell happened back there?" Christopher demanded.

"Chris, the guard made a move, man. It was either him or me, man." Lem answered.

"Fuck!" Christopher slammed his hand on the dashboard.

"You said, *'Don't think, just shoot.'* That's what I did. I didn't have a choice. He was going for his piece, man!" Lem grabbed the back of the head rest, pulling himself forward as he swung towards the side to emphasize his point into Christopher's ear.

Christopher took a deep breath and gritted his teeth. "I know. I know." *Dammit, this is going to be messy. This is bad ... really bad,* he thought.

***

"You seem extra agitated today, Christopher. Did something happen at work?" Dr. Grigsby asked.

"Yeah."

"Do you want to talk about it?"

"No."

"Well, what would you like to talk about?" She asked, peering over her glasses, staring at Christopher through his reflection.

Dr. Grigsby had turned her basement into a home office where she treated her patients. Dimly lit, it was a small space that didn't let in a lot of natural light but it served its purpose. She invested a little money to have it redecorated in a Victorian style. A big, chic, gold and burgundy Persian rug was sprawled in the middle of the floor on top of sleek oak hardwood floors. A cherrywood coffee table sat on top of the carpet with an expensive silver tea set for her clients to have their choice of tea or coffee. A gold, camelback sofa sat on one side of the coffee table and a tan chaise lounge sat on the other side. Another

Victorian balloon chair was stationed at one end of the coffee table. She usually sat at her big desk, which was always spotless, no papers, no files, not even one fingerprint. Her chair was a black rolling chair, standing out among the rest of the furniture. Next to her desk stood one single lamp.

Though she did have a desk, Dr. Grigsby preferred to let her patients stand, sit, or lay however they felt most comfortable talking. How was she supposed to get close to them, get inside their heads, if they were forced to sit stiffly across from her at her desk, made to feel like they were in the principal's office to be reprimanded for something? For Christopher, standing in front of her large wall mirror that hung above a cherry wood desk was most comfortable. He didn't like looking at Dr. Grigsby, looking back at him like he was some sort of spectacle, studying him, trying to pry inside his brain. He'd been seeing Dr. Grigsby for about three years, ever since he started getting in trouble with the law. The only reason he agreed to see a shrink was because it was part of his probation conditions. This was a small price to pay to remain a free man.

"Now we've been over this before, Chris. You know I'm here for you. We can waste the entire hour and just look at each other, or you can tell me what's bothering you." Christopher glared into the mirror at Dr. Grigsby, but said nothing. "Fine. Why don't we pick up where we last left off, then? You were expressing your feelings about your parents' friends."

Against his will, the mention brought out a light chuckle, "Oh yeah, I was telling you how much I hate rich people."

"And why do you hate rich people, Chris?"

"I don't know. I just do."

"Well, there must be some reason. Did any of your parents' friends ever do anything to you?"

"You mean like touch me *down there*?" He joked. "No." He said, rolling his eyes.

"I didn't necessarily mean sexually. I meant did they ever do anything to offend you? Make you feel bad? Something like that?"

"That's all those types of people are about. They say they like to make, and have, a lot of money to live well and to take care of their families, but really they just like to throw their money around to make people who have less than them feel inferior. That's why they don't deserve anything they have." He explained.

"Is that why you steal? You feel like you're taking back from the rich what they don't deserve to have?"

"I don't know what you're talking about." He responded crossly.

"Come on, Chris. Part of the reason you're here is because of your record. Theft, petty larceny, breaking and entering ... We both know your parents are well off and you don't need the money. So why do you do it?"

"Okay, fine. Maybe I do steal because I hate rich people. So, what? Just call me the modern-day Robin Hood." He smiled proudly. Dr. Grigsby looked back sternly with no reaction. "Lighten up. Jeez."

"Chris, I don't think you realize the seriousness of your crimes. You already have several strikes against you, most of which your parents have been able to make go away. But if you keep traveling down the path you're headed, the next time might be it. You could end up doing some serious time. Are you ready for that?"

"All that stuff is in the past. I'm on the straight and narrow now. You know that." He lied.

"Well, for your sake, I hope so." She pushed her glasses from the tip up to the bridge of her nose as she looked down at a small yellow pad. "Let's talk about your girlfriend."

"What about her?"

"How are things going with her? Rebecca, right?"

Christopher knew where this was headed and a hint of defensiveness crept into his voice. "Things are going fine."

"Last time we spoke you said she wanted to introduce you to her parents, but you weren't ready for that."

"Yeah ..."

"Well? Did she?"

"Nope."

"Still not ready, huh?"

"Look, I just don't want her getting all serious on me. I'm not ready to settle down yet, and if I meet her parents I know she's going to expect a ring, or something, next."

"I see. And why don't you feel like you're ready to settle down? You are young. Is that why?" Dr. Grigsby asked.

"Yeah, I'm young and I'm just not ready. I'm still ... How should I put it? ... Sowing my wild oats, if you know what I mean. I'm a man in demand and I don't need some little airhead weighing me down right now." He smiled arrogantly as he pretended to clean imaginary dirt from under his nails.

"Have you expressed these feelings to Rebecca?"

"I highly doubt telling my girlfriend she's an airhead I have no intention of settling down with is something she'd be too receptive of." He answered sarcastically.

"It might be hurtful but don't you think there's a nicer way you can let her down easy?"

"Let her down for what? Most women are airheads; so, if not her it'll just be someone else. Why pass up on that hot piece of ass?"

Dr. Grigsby raised an eyebrow and pinched her lips together before continuing, "Yes, you've mentioned her hotness several times in the past. Did you happen to bring in a picture of her this time? I'd love to see what she looks like."

"No, no picture. Carrying around a chick's picture is for saps."

"Chris," she started, deciding her next words carefully before treading. "Do you realize I've asked you to bring in a picture of Rebecca at least three times now? And each time you don't bring it, you have a different excuse?"

"I just told you. I'm not a sap. What do you want from me?" He barked, becoming agitated.

"I want you to tell the truth. It's okay, it's just you and me here. You don't have to make up stories for me."

"Make up stories? What stories?" He asked, confused.

"Just admit it. There really is no Rebecca. You made her up. She's a figment of your imagination."

Christopher stood silently for a moment, looking to be in deep thought, as though really trying to decide if what the doctor was saying rang any truth. "I don't know what you're getting at. Of course she's real! Do I look like a man who needs to lie? I get plenty of action. Why would I lie about my girlfriend? Just because I don't carry a picture around of her doesn't mean I'm a liar."

"I'm not calling you a liar. I'm simply suggesting that maybe your girlfriend isn't real. Maybe you just think she is."

"That doesn't make any sense, Dr. Grigsby."

"Tell me this, when and where was the last time you two went on a date?"

Christopher hesitated before answering, "I don't know. I guess it's been a while."

"Do you see my point?"

"No," he crossed his arms defiantly.

The session seemed to last longer than the allotted hour, but Christopher couldn't be happier when it finally ended. He headed for the front door to leave and, when he opened it, a lady jumped, startled, with her fist in the air as she prepared to knock.

"Sorry," Christopher said.

"Oh, that's okay," the woman grabbed her chest and exhaled with a short laugh. She eyed Christopher suspiciously like she recognized him from somewhere but wasn't sure. "Helen Grigsby?"

"Yes, this is the Grigsby residence. Dr. Grigsby is back in her office."

"Would you mind taking me back and showing me where it is?" The lady asked.

"Yeah, sure." There was something about the woman that struck Christopher as odd. Nevertheless, he turned on his heels to escort her back to Dr. Grigsby's office.

2 BHAVNA

"Yes! Yes! Harder! Harder!" Bhavna called out, her words streaming directly into Ashok's mouth, their faces barely touching. Ashok thrusted wildly into her as the bed creaked and groaned beneath them, joining in on the action. "Oh, Ashok," she moaned. "Yes, fuck me hard, baby!"

Ashok, seemingly distracted, banged his fist on the headboard, letting out a grunt of frustration. "I can't," he let out, breathless, as he rolled over onto his back. Bhavna could see his jaw tighten.

"What's wrong?" She propped herself onto her side, gently resting her hand on the mound of hair that centered in the middle of his chest.

"I don't know. I just can't." Ashok couldn't stand to look at her, feeling like less than a man. "Why do you have to talk like that, Bhavna?"

"Like what?"

"You know. All that dirty talk, using all those swear words. I don't like it."

Feeling embarrassed, Bhavna looked down. "I'm sorry. You're right." She paused for a moment, then began to stroke the patch of jet-black hair. "Try again?"

"No. It's almost time to go. We should start getting ready." He removed her hand from his chest, refusing to make eye contact. He rose and headed to the master bathroom, closing the door behind him.

Bhavna lay still, staring up at the ceiling, until she heard the water begin to spray against the shower curtain. She sat up and inhaled deeply, taking in the smell of sex mixed with the scent of cinnamon. The aroma lingered from an unlit Glade candle that sat on the edge of a massive mahogany dresser across from the foot of the bed. The room felt tight and bland with its vanilla walls. Bhavna's eyes fell on her own nude reflection from the mirror that was attached to the dresser. She gazed at the top half of her body with lust. Glancing at the digital clock that stood on the nightstand, she thought, *I can finish before he gets out of the shower.* Carefully and quietly she pulled out the bottom drawer. She reached her hand all the way towards the back, but still couldn't feel what she was looking for. She tugged on the drawer a little harder, almost pulling it out completely. Tucked in the rear, behind the drawer, she'd stashed a small, red, satin pouch with a drawstring.

There were several small items inside, but she felt around until her fingertips grazed the top of a vinyl case, the thing she knew would work fastest; her lifesaver. It was called that because it actually came in a tiny snap case that was designed with striped colors to look like the candy. She slid her hands over it, up and down a few times to warm it up. The buzzing sound was louder than she remembered once she gave the bottom a twist to turn it on. Eyes closed, she slowly rubbed it over each nipple just enough to graze them. They sprung up immediately and she moved on, lower. First, she placed the tip of the vibrator on the top of her clitoris, letting it sit there for a short moment before sliding it up and down against it. It wasn't long before she could hear the sticky sounds of her wetness as she continued sliding back and forth until she couldn't take it anymore.

She eased the tip of the vibrator inside of her, in and out, going in deeper with each stroke. The taste of blood mixed with her saliva as she bit down hard on her bottom lip to keep from moaning too loud. Ashok would have a fit if he found her pleasuring herself in such an open, shameless way. As her right hand went to work, faster and faster, shoving the plastic inside of her, she used her left hand to toss the blanket off of her. Her temperature rose, indicative of the heat she felt all over, as she looked down to see her hand moving rapidly. The sound of her moist juices splashing about only turned her on more and she tilted her head back while grabbing her left breast and squeezing hard. Her hips began to gyrate against the motion of her hand and her breathing turned shallow. Tucking both lips in, trying to maintain her discretion, she let out a half muffled moan as her body jerked and convulsed. Clear, wet, liquid squirted out all over, saturating the sheets and splashing onto her inner thigh.

Bhavna took a deep breath, and closed her eyes. Feeling slightly weakened from her six minutes of pleasure, she hated to move, and began to drift off easily. Moments later she heard the shower cut off, and she knew she couldn't linger much longer. She scrambled quickly to her feet, her toes meeting the abrasive, blonde, carpet of the floor. Stripping the bed sheets and tossing her lifesaver back into the bag, she thought, *I'll have to remember to clean it off later.* Then she stored it securely back in its hiding place.

Sliding into her plush cotton robe, she secured the belt around her waist as she called out down the hall, "Nirav! Zobia!" While she waited for a response, she slid her feet across the carpet, making her way to the walk-in closet. Running her hands over several plastic covered garments, she found the one she was looking for; a silk, gold, ankle-length dress. She found a matching red and gold dupatta to cover her shoulders. A small smile found its way on her face as she ran her hand over the dress, admiring it and picturing how beautiful she looked when trying it on in the boutique. She took a step back and called out to the children again, "Nirav! Zobia! Where are you? It's time to get ready for Mommy's concert!"

Ashok exited the bathroom, rubbing his head with a towel. He looked at Bhavna curiously, "Everything okay, sweetie?"

She smiled calmly, "Yes. I don't know what Nirav and Zobia

are up to, but they've got to start getting ready."

"Go ahead. You get ready for your big day. Don't worry about Nirav and Zobia." He said with a big smile, his mood vacated of prior frustrations.

"Thank you, my love." Bhavna returned his smile and planted a light kiss on his cheek before disappearing into the bathroom.

***

Eyelids closed but fluttering behind her circular framed glasses, Bhavna's upper torso gently and subtly jerked left, then right, with each stroke of her violin. A pianist plunked keys in the background, accompanying her. Lost to the melody of her solo, each long note vibrated through her core as she blocked out the entire outside world. The conductor waved his wand, mouthing the count as he focused on Bhavna. All eyes filling the concert hall were focused on Bhavna, her beauty stoic, arm moving with poise guiding each move of the bow, chin gracefully resting on the chin rest, cradling the neck of her instrument in the web of her hand. The silk fabric softly hugged her body while the dupatta hung loosely off of her shoulders; her dark hair neatly twisted and pinned upon the crown of her head.

Bhavna had been playing violin with the New York Multi-Cultural Orchestra for almost two years. Stephen LeFaire was the orchestra's conductor and she was his star pupil, quickly moving up the ranks to first chair. Spending countless hours together in practice, they shared a passionate love for music that few others understood. For Bhavna it was one of the only times she felt free. A person of few words, she was typically reserved and had a studious look about her. She spent most of her time behind the counter of Duane Reed as a pharmacist wearing her usual long white jacket. But playing with the orchestra was her time to shine. She seemed to feel more and more alive with each stroke of her bow, and she was undeniably talented.

She let off one last long fading note before breathing out and opening her eyes to the crowd. Applause erupted all around, enveloping her. She broke into a big grin and bowed her head. She gave a half curtsey before returning to her seat, joining her fellow orchestra members who gave whispers of a job well done. Looking out into the concert hall, she could see little hands waving excitedly at her from the second row. She waved back to Nirav and Zobia, blowing them kisses, and Ashok smiled proudly as he continued to clap with everyone else.

"Bhavna, spectacular! Simply spectacular!" Stephen beamed from ear to ear as he cupped Bhavna's hand inside of his, then proceeded to kiss her once on each cheek. Other audience members greeted their loved ones after the concert was over, and the hall cleared out slowly. You could see flowers and balloons being toted throughout.

"Thank you, Stephen. I could not have done it without you."

"Honey, very nice show." Ashok approached the pair.

"Bhavna, dear, I have something for you." Stephen lifted a long white box with a red ribbon sitting, balanced atop one of the flip-down seats.

Bhavna glanced at an empty-handed Ashok in embarrassment. "Oh Stephen, you shouldn't have went through the trouble." She said, nervously.

"Trouble? No trouble at all for my star! Wasn't she just simply wonderful, Ashok?" Stephen was giddy. At fifty-two, he was nearly twenty years older than Bhavna and his head full of white hair made it no secret. Although his look was distinguished, like a fine aged wine, his spirit was that of a young person.

"Yes, I enjoyed it very much." Ashok replied, also embarrassed by Stephen's brazen display of admiration that read far more than that of mentor to mentee.

"We're all going to Giovanni's as soon as everyone clears out. Who's up for Italian?" Stephen said, excitedly.

Bhavna looked away before answering, "Thank you, Stephen, but I don't think so. We really should be getting home." She motioned towards Zobia and Nirav who quietly stood by Ashok's side.

"What? What's a celebration without the star of the night?" Stephen pressed insistently.

"It's fine, honey. You go on ahead. I have some work I need to catch up on anyway."

"Ashok, are you sure you won't come? If only for a little while?" She asked with a slight twinge of disappointment in her tone.

"No, you go ahead with your friends, Bhavna. Really, it's fine. You and I can celebrate tomorrow, maybe?" Ashok purposely added a dash of hope to his voice.

"Okay, tomorrow." Bhavna smiled. "I will be home soon. Don't you stay up too late." She cautioned the children.

"Yes, Mommy," she heard the reply of small voices.

Once Ashok and the children headed out the double doors, Stephen hooked his arm through Bhavna's as they began to walk towards the stage. "Well, aren't you going to open it?" He asked referring to the box she carried.

"Oh, yes. Yes, of course." She smiled nervously as she lifted the lid to find six red long stemmed roses. "Oh, Stephen, you shouldn't have. They are so beautiful. They really are. Thank you."

"You're very welcome." Stephen held his head high and grinned proudly.

***

Bhavna held a distaste for alcohol but, at Stephen's persistence, she was on her third glass of Spottswoode Cabernet Sauvignon when he called for a champagne toast. Seated around their grandiose table in the back private room of Giovanni's was the usual, carefully selected, orchestra elites, as well as a few of Stephen's friends he'd invited. Giovanni's was a top-notch restaurant with a long history of serving New York City's most sophisticated. The private room was dimly lit with cream-colored candles that flickered from their sconces that were fixed to the walls. Not a single crease was detected on the crisp, bleach-white, table cloth. Black and white autographed photos of celebrities dating back to the early 1900's lined the walls. The rough sound of the sturdy, wooden, chairs sliding over the deep red Spanish tiles of the floor could be heard throughout the night.

Each person delicately held their bubbly-filled flute as they awaited Stephen's toast. He'd spared no expense, as always, ordering a bottle of Dom Perignon. Bhavna was more relaxed than she cared to be, her dupatta fallen completely off of her shoulders, just barely hanging on at the elbows. The spaghetti straps of her dress showed more skin than she would normally care to but the red wine had her moving in slow motion. She, too, held her champagne glass but with no intentions of actually drinking it.

"Thank you all for making this night a success. Because of you the New York Multi-Cultural Orchestra has reached a level of perfection beyond my wildest desires. We did so well tonight, the concert hall has invited us back to play in the fall. What do you think of that?" Stephen paused to allow for a mixture of applause and excited acknowledgements at the news. "I would like to extend a special thank you to Jim. You were exceptional." Jim, the pianist, nodded and lifted his glass in acknowledgement while others lent their approval through smiles. "And of course, I couldn't complete this toast without giving an extra special thank you to Miss Bhavna Patel on violin. You were phenomenal tonight, darling." He said, looking down at Bhavna who sat directly next to him, smiling, trying to hide the effect the wine was having on her. "So, without further ado, to the orchestra and to Bhavna! Cheers!" Everyone raised their glasses and clinked with one another around the table.

Once back in his seat, Stephen eyed Bhavna seductively. Though she was oblivious. With his index finger he made an imaginary trail down her bare shoulder and to her lap, stopping at her knee. She looked shyly out the corner of her eye, then tried to focus on the plate of eggplant parmesan sitting in front of her. He continued to rub her knee for a moment, testing the waters, before slowly pinching the silk fabric, causing the hemline to rise slowly, inch by inch, until he reached a bare knee.

Bhavna swallowed hard, still looking down.

"Bhavna, honey, you didn't drink your champagne." He purred in her ear so others wouldn't hear. Though everyone else was so excited about the news that they were wrapped up in their own conversations anyway. All except one.

"Oh no! We can't have that! You're the lady of the night. It just wouldn't be right if you didn't have at least a sip of champagne." Carl chimed in, eyeing Stephen with a devilish look.

"Bhavna, this is my friend Carl. We used to work the stockroom floor together on Wall Street." Stephen explained.

"Nice to meet you, Carl." Bhavna replied.

"The pleasure is all mine. I really loved your performance tonight." He whispered in her other ear as she sat sandwiched between the two.

"Thank you."

"You're welcome, dear. Now ... how about that champagne?" he leaned in with a grin.

"I don't know. I've already had three glasses of wine."

"Yeah, but that's not champagne. You have to at least try the champagne. We just won't take 'no' for an answer. Will we, Stephen?" He pushed.

Bhavna felt her cheeks warm as Stephen inched his way up her inner thigh under the table. She released a short, light breath, "Well, okay. Maybe just a little."

"That a girl," Carl coaxed as he began to trace Bhavna's hairline along the nape of her neck.

Once dinner was over, everyone said their goodbyes, some giving staged hugs and others air kisses to each cheek as if they were all somewhere other than New York City. Bhavna looped her arm through Stephen's for discreet support. Making their way towards the front exit of Giovanni's, Stephen cooed into Bhavna's eardrum.

"Bhavna, my dear, you look more beautiful than ever tonight. Please, let me see you home?" Stephen held Bhavna's coat slung over his arm. What was left of an earlier snowfall crunched beneath their feet.

"Sure, Stephen. That would be fine." She answered. They stood on the street while Stephen hailed a black stretch limo he had on standby. The cool air stung their faces. A gust of wind grazed Bhavna's shoulders. She smiled, welcoming the freezing chill that ran up her spine, causing the back of her neck to feel all prickly.

"Ah, let me warm you up...since Stephen seems to be holding your coat hostage." A voice crept to her neck from behind and hands started to rub her arms up and down. It was Carl.

"Oh," Bhavna, slightly startled, smiled uncomfortably at him.

"Carl is going to share the limo with us. You don't mind." Stephen suggestively asked.

"No – no, I don't mind, Stephen."

"Don't worry. I don't bite." Carl stepped around to face Bhavna and winked.

Carl wasn't the best looking man. He wasn't hideous either. He could benefit from a gym membership judging by the way his stomach threatened to burst through the cummerbund he wore. His skin was pink and splotchy. His teeth were yellowing behind raw lips, and his toilet bowl ring of hair told his age. He wasn't Stephen.

The limo pulled up. The driver stepped out and opened the door. "Ladies first!" Stephen smiled and bowed with his arm outstretched.

Bhavna climbed in and sat her small, sequin, purse on the seat next to her. Next, Stephen folded in and sat with his thigh touching hers, extending his arm around her shoulders. Carl made his way in and sat on the seat directly across from the duo, stretching one hand across the back of the seat and using the other to loosen his bow tie. He seemed anxious, excited about something. Even though no words had been spoken, a full set of buttery teeth shown from ear to ear.

"Carl, will you relax? You're going to make her nervous for Christ's sakes!" Stephen chuckled as he stroked Bhavna's shoulder.

"I'm sorry, Bhavna. I don't mean to make you uncomfortable. You must understand, I'm just astounded by your beauty."

Bhavna engaged Carl's gaze briefly, then quickly averted her eyes. "Thank you. Really, it's okay." Carl wasn't as handsome or charming as Stephen, but he would do, Bhavna thought.

"Here, let me help you get more comfortable." Stephen seductively slid her dupatta through her elbows, tossing it on an empty space next to Carl where he'd already tossed her coat. Bhavna looked out at the city lights twinkling against the black New York sky. "It is beautiful. Isn't it?" Stephen whispered in her ear.

"Yes, very."

Stephen couldn't wait any longer and from the looks of it, neither could Carl. He placed one hand gently around the front of her neck, leaving her with no choice but to meet him eye-to-eye. Bhavna allowed her eyes to close, engaging in a passionate kiss. Stephen's mouth was comfortable and familiar to her. He desired her in a different way than Ashok did. There was something deeper, a fire that only they shared. But tonight, they would extend that passion to Carl.

Carl watched like a teen boy who'd just hit puberty as Stephen savored each taste of Bhavna's tongue. He ran his fingers up to her head, releasing the bun that sat atop. A blanket of dark wavy strands fell to her waist. After running his fingers through it several strokes, he then proceeded to pull one spaghetti strap down to allow one of Bhavna's swollen breasts to make its way out the top of her dress. She didn't care. She wanted it to happen. She wanted Carl to watch, taking a moment to open an eye to show him her approval of his stare. She tugged on the other strap, trying to get it down too.

Stephen grabbed her hand and kissed it. "Easy. Let me help you with that." He unzipped the back of the dress so that the top half came folding forward, exposing both breasts. He cupped one in his large palm, greedily devouring as much flesh as he could fit into his mouth. Carl came out of his suit jacket and unbuttoned his pants as he began to shamelessly rub his bulge, never taking his eyes from the scene unfolding before him. Bhavna had no idea where the driver was taking them and she didn't care. Everything about this moment felt right. Every intimate moment with Stephen felt inexplicably right.

Stephen's hands roamed all over, one finding its way up her dress caressing her thighs. Bhavna tilted her head back and let out a soft moan, letting Carl know that Stephen had found her center of ecstasy. Carl could see Stephen's elbow moving back and forth between her legs, wishing it was he in that position instead. Still, he waited patiently. Bhavna's moans continued until her body jerked and a devilish grin crept across her face. She was just getting started. She grabbed Stephen around the neck with both hands and kissed him hard. One of her lean legs swung over his lap as she straddled him like a wild cowgirl.

He exchanged no words but instead let out a sinister laugh of approval as he hiked the silk fabric up to her waist. Her full petite bottom was now exposed to Carl as she waited for Stephen to unzip his slacks. He barely had his member out before she pounced, mounting him before bouncing steadily up and down like a trained jockey. As the momentum built she let out a growl. Her hair brushed up and down against her backside and she attempted to swing her head to flip it to one side. Stephen had other plans though. As she continued galloping, he gathered her hair into his fist, wrapping it around his hand once before yanking her head backward. She let out a laughter-moan combination before raising both of her hands up to the roof of the limo. She didn't stop there. Her hands reached back and back until they were flatly planted on the floor, her waist still fused to Stephen, her torso bridged with such a skilled arch in her back and her head dangling upside down, inches from the carpeted floor. The bottom half of her body still faced Stephen, but her upper half flexed backward so that her face looked at Carl. Her inverted face beckoned him. "Your turn," she let out.

Carl's brow became a wrinkle of confusion as Stephen continued thrusting his hips upwards, causing Bhavna's twins to bounce, teasing him. Bhavna licked her lips, signaling to Carl what she wanted. His face flushed crimson for a brief moment as his two brains made the connection. In a fast hurry, he whipped out his throbbing manhood, not wanting to miss out on this opportunity for participation. He crouched so that his knees met the carpet and his waist was leveled to Bhavna's dangling face. Steadying himself, he entered her welcoming mouth timidly.

Bhavna's neck feverishly went to work jerking back and forth, quickly putting Carl at ease with her showcase of skill. Stephen, witnessing Carl's astoundment, let out a wild cackle. Carl returned an unsure chortle as he began to relax and enjoy the moment. After both men released, Stephen had the driver drop Carl off at his home. He and Bhavna continued their ride of pleasure, going for rounds two, three, and four before their night together finally ended.

The light whistle of Ashok's snoring stirred Bhavna awake. She rolled over to find him flat on his back. The morning sunlight just barely began to peek through the blinds. She cupped the side of her head, trying to remember the previous night's events. She found it difficult to recall how she'd even made it back home and into bed. Her eyes searched the room for clues, but found none. They landed on her lifesaver sitting on top of her nightstand. *Had she gone for another round with herself?* Embarrassed, she quietly slid open the nightstand drawer and placed it inside. She took another scan of the room, wondering where her dress was. It wouldn't have been unlike Ashok to wait up for her when she stayed out late like this. Assuming he'd probably caught her stumbling on her way in and, so as not to wake the children, he got her changed and safely tucked into bed.

***

Dr. Grigsby's office was quiet, except for the hum of a small white fan that oscillated from the corner of the room. Bhavna lay on the chaise lounge chair staring up at the ceiling as she listened to Dr. Grigsby's soothing voice.

"You're still seeing Stephen," she stated.

Bhavna sighed and closed her eyes, "Yes".

"And what about Ashok? What if he finds out?"

Bhavna whined. "I knowww. I knowww. But it's so different with Stephen. We have a special connection."

"Bhavna, that's the same thing you said about Thomas, Nick, and Cole. We've talked about this before. You know this type of erratic behavior is unhealthy and dangerous."

"But I can't help it. I think about sex all the time, Dr. Grigsby. It's like there's a fire down in me that I can't put out no matter how hard I try."

"Have you tried any of the methods we've discussed?"

"Yes. Yes, of course. I have more toys than my two children combined. I use them, but it's never enough."

"Speaking of your children, how are they? How are they recovering from the incident?"

"They're fine. They don't say much about it. I've explained to them that Mommy is sick."

"And do you think your continued behavior is conducive to their well-being?"

"I know it's not, Dr. Grigsby. I was mortified when they walked in on Russell and me. I don't think I've ever been so embarrassed in my life." Bhavna squeezed her eyelids tight and rubbed with her fingertips, trying to erase the memories.

"Bhavna, in the past three years that I've been treating you, you've been arrested for solicitation once, indecent exposure four times, have had one unplanned pregnancy, and contracted two STDs. Clearly you have to see how your uncontrolled sexual behavior is harmful to both you and your family." Dr. Grigsby stressed her words.

"I know," she groaned. "I don't want to be like this, Dr. Grigsby. Do you think I *choose* to be a sex addict?"

"I know you don't. I just don't understand. For a while there I thought we were making progress. It's been three months with no arrests. You said the self-stimulation techniques were working. Have you still been attending your meetings?"

"Yes, but lately ... I'm not feeling fulfilled. Ashok is just so plain and boring in bed. He gets upset with the language I use or whenever I come on to him. He says the man is supposed to be the only initiator of sex. Sometimes I feel like he's punishing me by withholding. Then I joined the orchestra and that helped to redirect my focus, but Stephen took such a special interest in me. We got close and things just got out of control I guess."

"You *guess*?"

"I *know*."

"Bhavna, I just don't want things to get so out of control to where you can no longer handle everything. Today it's only Stephen but you know how quickly that can progress to more. You know you're lucky you were picked up for solicitation those times. You could've easily been raped or murdered. There's a lot of dangerous predators out there. I just don't want to see you go down that road again, having sex with random strangers in random places. It's just not safe. Do you understand that, Bhavna?"

Salty tears began to stream down the corner of Bhavna's eyes back into her hair. She thought back to all the Johns she'd engaged with, not even for money, but just for sexual fulfillment. No matter how many, it never seemed to be enough. Her children had already witnessed her having sex with Russell, the cable man, in their laundry room. Ashok was the most understanding man she could ask for. He'd forgiven her time and time again and supported her throughout her therapy. Had they been back in their old country, he would've disowned her by now; and it would've been justified. And to repay him, what did she do? Start the whole cycle all over again with Stephen.

Bhavna wanted desperately to be a good woman to Ashok. They'd been married since she was sixteen. Despite his parents' objections of marrying a woman of a lower class, Ashok loved Bhavna. He defied his parents, and in doing so, gave Bhavna and her family a better life. When they moved to the states, that life became even better than she could ever imagine. She was eternally grateful to Ashok and she did love him. She just couldn't control her raging hormones and, even worse, she didn't know why.

Even now as she lay in Dr. Grigsby's office being scolded by the doctor, all she could think of was visiting the Swing House. The Swing House was an open market sex club that Stephen had introduced her to. Strangers traveled from all over the city to the shady little spot in the village to have sex anonymously with strangers, fulfilling some of their wildest fantasies. What she was doing felt wrong. Still, Bhavna would find herself at the Swing House before the night was over.

3 JESSICA

"You know the police are still asking to speak with you, Helen." Dr. Planthers informed. Dr. Grigsby sat with her friend in a small café near a giant window in Midtown. Both gripped warm foam cups of latte as they people-watched.

"Oh, what for?" She sighed in annoyance.

"You know why. They have questions about the robberies."

"I don't know what they expect *me* to tell them. I don't know anything." She looked bewildered as she took in a deep gasp, her chest rising, eyes widened, chin tilted down in defense.

"They want to know about Christopher." Dr. Planthers replied softly as she searched Dr. Grigsby's expression. Dr. Grigsby's eyes darted about to avoid making direct eye contact.

"I have a doctor-patient confidentiality to uphold. *You* should know that better than anyone, Marge."

Doctor Planthers grew quiet for a few moments as she studied Dr. Grigsby, deciding carefully what to say next. She didn't want to agitate her. "Well, maybe *we* could talk about Christopher." She suggested. "Helen, I'm worried for your safety."

"James! Mocha latte with caramel and whipped cream!" The cashier behind the counter called out to patrons waiting for their hot drinks. A short bald man rushed forward to claim his foam cup, dropping some coins into a tip jar that sat near the register.

After turning to look towards the yelling cashier, lingering purposely for seconds after to avoid the conversation, Dr. Grigsby slowly turned back around. "Worried for my safety?" She waved, immediately dismissing the idea as her face cringed. "Honestly, Marge, you're so dramatic. There's nothing to be worried about. I really think I'm making progress with Christopher." She lied.

"Helen, a man was shot and nearly killed in that last robbery Upstate!" She forcefully hissed.

"And what's that got to do with Christopher? You don't know that he had anything to do with that just like I don't know." Dr. Grigsby's eyes finally met Dr. Planthers' with a glare as she crossed her arms.

"I've seen the police sketch ... They've identified a suspect." She kept her voice hushed in an attempt to calm Dr. Grigsby and not draw attention.

Dr. Grigsby's face froze, unblinking. "Have you noticed anything different about me?" She broke into a smile and shook her head lightly, causing her hair to swing across her back.

"Uh ye-yes. You've done something ... *different* to your hair." Dr. Planthers searched for the right words as she fumbled through her purse to get to a small pad and pen. She scribbled something quickly and threw it back in the big tote.

"Ugh! You and that pad! You must take that thing with you everywhere you go. Yes, my hair!" She exclaimed before cupping her hand to the side of her mouth in an exaggerated whisper, "They're extensions." The former brunette now sported a shiny jet-black weave, curtesy of the small hair combs discretely secured in throughout her dyed mane. The long strands cascaded down the back of the grey pea coat she wore. "Well ... what do you think?" She perkily asked, her eyes bright as she waited for the doctor's response, filled with the excitement of a puppy's wagging tail.

"It's ... definitely a different look for you. I'm just so used to seeing you with the brown hair." She had a hard time trying to find something nice to say about it. To her, it didn't look good. It looked ... ridiculous ... fake ... unrealistic. It looked as though Dr. Grigsby was trying to be someone other than herself.

After meeting with Dr. Planthers, Dr. Grigsby had plans for an early dinner with Claude. She'd been seeing Claude for a little more than a year and things were going well. She hoped he would finally be the one to pop the question, settle down with, and have some children. At age thirty-eight, she knew the clock was ticking but still remained optimistic about her future.

Claude was different. He was patient and supportive, unlike many of her previous romantic interests. He understood her love and devotion to her patients where others didn't. His eyes showed empathy with every gaze and he displayed a genuine concern for her well-being. The pair met at a psychiatric fundraiser that Dr. Planthers hosted at her office. The two bonded over a bidding war for an antique ship in a bottle. Claude won and graciously gifted it to Dr. Grigsby. They hit it off immediately.

She smiled to herself as she sat on the train in route to Claude's work. It was the sudden feeling that someone was watching her that snagged Dr. Grigsby out of her nostalgic daydream. She looked up to see a woman seated diagonally across from her quickly glance away. When she looked down towards the end of the train she could feel the woman's eyes back on her. She turned fast, catching the woman's stare before she diverted her eyes again. This went on for the duration of the ride until the woman's stop came up. She folded her newspaper underneath her arm, glancing once more at Dr. Grigsby as she passed before trotting through the train doors.

Claude waited outside of the tall skyscraper where he worked for a software company as a support analyst. His coat collar stood turned up, protecting the back of his neck from the winter air. He was a tall lean man. His large ears could be seen peeking out the top of his coat, the tips red. His gloved hands were shoved deep into his pockets until he brought them out to place them on Dr. Grigsby's shoulders. This was their way of greeting. He'd place his hands on top of her shoulders while she remained arm's length away. They would smile sincerely and gaze into each other's eyes before releasing. Kissing and hugging like other couples was a foreign concept to them.

"Helen, my love, I thought you'd never get here. Let's hurry. It's freezing!" White puffs of cold breath escaped into the air. He was giddy. She looped her arm through his and off they went scurrying down the city's cold street.

Once inside the restaurant, Claude removed a handkerchief and proceeded to wipe down both seats. He reached inside his interior jacket pocket to retrieve a small bottle of hand sanitizer. "Have some?" He posed it as a question but Dr. Grigsby knew it was more of a heavy suggestion.

"Sure," she extended her palm across the table for him to ooze a cool drop into her hand.

While they waited for the waiter, Claude rearranged the condiments alongside of the table so that the bottles and shakers were in order from tallest to shortest. Then he aligned the wine menu so that it stood neatly in the same line as the condiments but perfectly centered on their table. Dr. Grigsby thought his Obsessive-Compulsive Disorder was cute and sat there waiting patiently with her hands clasped in her lap. Next, Claude asked for a cup of hot water and an additional napkin. One was to wash and dry the silverware and the other would be for his lap. This was his ritual each time they dined.

"I still don't know what made you do that to your hair." He swirled around red wine in a glass as they waited for their meal.

"You don't like it? I think it looks ... *exotic*."

"Oh, it's not that I don't like it, honey. I guess it will just take some getting used to. That's all." He smiled a warm smile. "You know I think you're beautiful no matter what you do to your hair."

"Really? Even if I shave it bald?" She teased.

"Even if you shave it bald." Then he quickly added, as if afraid she might actually do it, "But please don't." During the time they'd been dating, Dr. Grigsby was known to change her hairstyles like one changes underwear. It was always something drastic, and without warning. It was as though she purposely wanted to shock people. One time she actually cut her hair stunningly short. Everyone but her found it mannish, but no one had the guts to say so aloud. Her plethora of hairdos included everything from dying her hair bleach blonde to sporting a set of ridiculous cornrows.

After dinner, they took a stroll down to the subway and Claude escorted Dr. Grigsby back home. Once again, he placed his hands on her shoulders gazing deeply with loving eyes.

"Call me when you get in?" She said.

"Of course." As he walked down the front steps, he turned midway and blew a kiss. "Night!"

Feeling light and bubbly inside, she closed her front door behind her, and leaned her back against it, tilting her head back with her eyes closed. She exhaled before opening them, then made her way towards the kitchen. She flicked on the light as she passed through the living room, glancing briefly in the big mirror that hung on the wall just opposite the couch. She doubled back immediately, her heart thumping loudly.

"*Jessica*!" She was startled by the young teen sitting quietly on her couch.

"*Helen*," she answered crossly. Her arms followed suit, as did the glare on her face. "I've been waiting to talk to you for almost an hour." Her voice was flat and cold.

"We've talked about this before, Jessica. You can't just show up here and ... *break* into my home!"

"Oh, don't get your panties in a bunch. I didn't break in. I used the spare key you keep under the flower pot on the side of the house. You know, you really should be more discreet with that, Helen." She patronized.

"That's the fifth time I've had to move that key and, please, call me Dr. Grigsby. Haven't we talked about that several times also, Jessica?" She chastised as though speaking to a four-year-old instead of the sixteen-year-old blonde who'd just trespassed into her home.

"Why can't I call you Helen? That's your name, isn't it? You call me Jessica."

"Yes, but I'm your therapist, not one of your classmates.

Remember we talked about setting and respecting boundaries?" The doctor asked.

"Whatever," Jessica rolled her eyes and ran her fingers through her long, stringy, ponytail. "Where were you? Out with your boyyyfriiiend?" She teased.

"Yes. As a matter of fact, I was, but you're not here to talk about me. Why don't you tell me what you're here to talk about?" Dr. Grigsby walked into the kitchen to begin making herself a cup of hot tea as Jessica's voice followed.

"Why do you think I'm here?" She answered sarcastically. "I'm here to talk ... about ... an urge." She wrung her hands in her lap and looked down with embarrassment.

"What kind of urge? To use or...?"

"The other urge," her voice was low.

"Tell me more. What brought about the urge this time, Jessica?" The doctor coaxed.

Jessica shrugged and mumbled in response, "I don't know ... but I'm in a lot of trouble."

"Trouble? Why? Why don't you take me step by step and tell me what happened? Would you like some tea? It's peppermint."

"No." Jessica grew quiet for a few minutes while she gathered her thoughts, trying to make sense of what she was about to disclose to the doctor.

Dr. Grigsby had been treating Jessica for two years. She was a troubled teen, shipped back and forth from foster homes and group homes from the time her mother overdosed on heroine and died. She was only eight at the time. Now she'd been ordered by a judge to attend therapy after her last run-in with the law. She'd been busted for the possession of cocaine. In their sessions, Jessica confessed to Dr. Grigsby about her habits. She smoked marijuana regularly, dabbled in methamphetamines, and sniffed cocaine fairly often when things weren't going well in her life. Dr. Grigsby had been trying to talk Jessica into getting into a treatment program, but she knew it would only be successful if it was her own choice. The drugs weren't her only vice, though.

"I was babysitting for Mrs. Meyers again yesterday." She

stopped talking.

"And?" Dr. Grigsby immediately grew worried. Jessica also had prior records for child abuse and child endangerment. Just being around children alone was a violation of her probation.

"She said she only needed me to watch Martin for about an hour. She shouldn't have left me alone with him for more than an hour." She whined as she began to build her case.

"Just calm down and tell what happened, Jessica." The doctor instructed in a steady voice.

"Mrs. Meyers said she only needed me to watch Martin for an hour while she went to the pharmacy and grocery store to pick up a couple of things. She was going to pay me twenty dollars and I needed the money; so, I said yes. So, it was just the two of us in the apartment, just me and Martin."

"Go on," the doctor coaxed.

"At first everything was fine. Then, after the hour passed, Martin started getting restless. He wouldn't go to sleep even though he was sleepy. He started to cry and he just wouldn't stop." Jessica's voice began to shake.

"How old is Martin?"

"He's one and a half. He's walking now but not really talking just yet." She explained as she began to crack her knuckles, a habit that surfaced whenever she talked about something that was really difficult for her to express.

"Okay, go on."

"Well, he wouldn't shut up!" Her pale white face turned red as her eyes began to well up. It was as if she was reliving the experience again. "I tried everything. I gave him his favorite snack, the animal crackers. I put on cartoons. I held him, rocked him. I sang to him. Nothing would shut the little brat up!" She huffed and crossed her arms.

"So, what did you do, Jessica?" Jessica just bit her lower lip and began to slowly bend her middle finger backwards. "You can tell me. Come on. What did you do to Martin?"

"I – I ... it wasn't my fault!" She blurted out as she burst into tears and leaned over, putting her head in her hands. "It wasn't my fault, Dr. Grigsby! You gotta believe me! He just wouldn't stop crying!"

"I know. Calm down. I can't help you if you don't tell me what happened, Jessica."

Jessica began taking heavy short breaths as she tried to regain control over herself. "I grabbed him and slammed him on the bed. Then ... I ... took a small pillow – it was a real small pillow, Dr. Grigsby. I promise it was small. I didn't think anything would happen. I just wanted him to be quiet." She paused and took a deep breath.

"Then what happened? What did you do with the pillow?"

"I put it over his face and I held it there. He started kicking and grabbing my hands but I just wanted his crying to stop so I just held the pillow there until he stopped moving." She stopped to sniffle and wipe the tears from her face. "When I took the pillow off, he was all blue and he wasn't breathing anymore. I didn't know what to do!"

"So, what *did* you do?"

"I called 9-1-1. Once they said an ambulance was on the way, I tried to give him mouth to mouth but nothing was happening. He still wasn't breathing. So, I hurried and put him in his crib."

"Oh my god. Jessica, where is Martin now? What happened to Martin?" Dr. Grigsby asked.

"He's fine. They were able to resuscitate him at the hospital and they sent him home with Mrs. Meyers. They asked me a lot of questions."

"What did you tell them?" Dr. Grigsby had a horrified look on her face although she was relieved to hear that the child was okay.

"I lied, Dr. Grigsby. I told them that Martin was taking a nap in the crib and that when I went up to check on him he just wasn't breathing. I'm not sure if they believed me." She speculated.

"Jessica, you know children should not be under your care. We've talked about this several times. Why did you agree to watch Martin?"

Jessica shifted in her seat, crossing her legs before she answered. "I don't know. I needed the money. I needed a fix."

Her voice lowered in shame and she began cracking her knuckles again. "She was only supposed to be gone an hour."

"Jessica, do you know what Munchausen Syndrome is?"

"No, why? Do you think I have that?" She questioned.

"Possibly. This is not the first child to stop breathing while in your care, Jessica. In two of your child endangerment cases, the children stopped breathing. Isn't that correct?"

"Yeah, but those weren't my fault either. I didn't do anything to those kids. I saved them! If I hadn't gotten them to the hospital in time, they would've died but they didn't." She defended herself. "Besides, nobody was ever able to prove I'd done anything to those kids anyway."

"Just because it wasn't proven doesn't mean it didn't happen." The doctor tried to be gentle in her accusation.

"What are you trying to say, doctor?" Jessica stood up, glaring at the doctor.

"People with Munchausen Syndrome oftentimes fake illnesses or disease in order to gain attention and sympathy from others." Dr. Grigsby explained.

"Well, I haven't faked any illnesses; so, I guess that means I don't have it." She retorted.

"Sometimes the person will inflict disease or illness on a loved one or someone under their care because through making them sick or injured, they can gain that same sympathy just by being involved as the caretaker. It's called Munchausen Syndrome by Proxy." Jessica plopped back down in her seat and looked out the front window, ashamed to face her demons. "Jessica, how did it make you feel when the doctors and nurses were asking you questions about Martin?"

Jessica shrugged, letting her shoulders hunch. "I don't know."

"Did you feel happy? Sad? Angry? Nervous?"

"I don't know. I guess I felt ... comforted." She confessed.

"Comforted?"

"Yeah. I mean nobody ever checks on me or asks how I'm doing. I'm in this world all alone, you know?" Her voice cracked as she spoke. "It's nice when the doctors and nurses come around you to ask how you're doing, tell you you did the right thing bringing the kid to the hospital or calling 9-1-1 or whatever. They offer me stuff like snacks and soda and tell me everything is going to be okay and not to worry. It makes me feel safe."

"I see ... Jessica, I think we made some big progress today. By opening up and being honest with me – and yourself, I think we're starting to get to the root of some of your issues. But I need you to schedule an appointment and come back, okay?"

"Okay," Jessica agreed, reluctantly.

"And Jessica?"

"Yeah?" she answered.

"Please, stay away from kids. If anyone asks you to babysit just say no." Jessica nodded as she got up slowly to prepare for her departure. "And no more breaking into my house!"

4 YOLANDA

Yolanda shifted her weight back and forth, her hands stuffed down into her jean pockets, as she waited impatiently in the busy 34th Street McDonalds. The fast food restaurant was jammed packed, as always. She hated this place, but she was hungry and she only had thirty minutes to grab something before catching the subway to her appointment.

She stood in one of the six long lines looking up at the menu. There was nothing on it that she really wanted, but she knew she had to pick something. Just then she felt the back of her Timberland boot being crushed against her heel. The man standing in line behind her clearly didn't know the boundaries of personal space. Sure, the place was wall to wall packed but breathing down Yolanda's neck wasn't going to make the line move any faster.

Yolanda took pride in her appearance, always wearing the latest in what the fashion editors were now calling "urban" gear, and she kept her boots clean. Her temperature began to boil as she quickly spun around, "Aye, man! What'chu doin'? You not even gon' say excuse me? You just stepped on my shit!" Her eyebrows were pulled down low in a scowl.

"I sorry," the man apologized in a choppy accent.

"Oh, *you sorry*," She mocked. "Next time watch where the fuck you goin'! I swear you just got off the boat muthafuckas always breathing down a bitch back. Don't y'all know what personal space is?" She spat. She mumbled before rolling her eyes and turning back around, "shit." Because no one wanted to get into their own beef, everyone just looked on with side glances in an attempt to appear as though they weren't paying attention.

As the line continued to inch forward, the man was sure to keep his distance behind Yolanda. It was too late, however. The match was already lit and the fuse was about to be blown. "Aye-o! Can y'all hurry this line the fuck up?" She yelled towards the row of cashiers that were working feverishly. "Damn! How hard is it to put a burger and some fries in a bag? Y'all act like y'all back there performing brain surgery or something." No one responded.

Something about Yolanda's presence was intimidating. The wall furthest from the exit had a big mirror that ran the length of the wall. It was just above one of the two seating areas. A case of metal stairs led to the other seating are. Yolanda glanced in the mirror to check herself out. Her chocolate skin was smooth with not a blemish in site. One would think she gave herself facials daily, but not Yolanda. Yolanda wasn't that kind of woman. Her shoulder length cornrows ran neatly down the back of her head. A tan bandana folded into a three-inch band was tied around her edges. She wore an oversized off-white long john thermal shirt underneath a wheat-colored vest. The vest matched the wheat-colored boots she wore. Her dark and baggy denim jeans were neatly cuffed and sat over the leather ankle of the boot. A thick platinum chain adorned her neck, resting on her chest, her C-cup boobs taped down with athletic tape under the sports bra she wore. Her walk was pimped and that was even evident in the slow way she crept along with the rest of the patrons towards the front of the line until it was finally her turn.

"Welcome to McDonalds. May I take your order?" The young cashier said, blandly, as though this were her thousandth time saying it that day. Given the bustling location, it probably was.

"Yeah, let me get a uhhh ..." Yolanda stared back up to the menu overhead as she took her time deciding. "Let me get a uhhh ... A number one with – wait hold up!" She changed her mind, "Nah, let me get a uhhh –"

She was cut short by the cashier sucking her teeth and briskly turning her back to continue working while Yolanda made up her mind. She pulled some items from the food belt and walked over to the fry station to drop two sacks of fries into a bag. "Two quarter pounders with cheese and two fries!" The cashier called out.

"Excuse me," A lady squeezed next to Yolanda, grabbing the bag that sat on the counter next to the register.

"Are you ready?" The cashier asked impatiently.

"Yeah. Just gimme a chicken sandwich with fries."

"A McChicken with fries," the cashier said aloud as she tapped buttons on her screen. "Grilled or fried?"

"Huh?" Yolanda was confused by the option.

The girl spoke slowly, insulting Yolanda. "Do – you – want – the chick-en sand-which fried or grilled?"

"Aye-o don't get smart. It ain't my fault you work here. Fried."

The girl stared in response. "What size?"

"I don't know – large."

"For here or to go?"

"Oh my god," Yolanda huffed, annoyed by all the questions. "Make it to go."

"Anything else?"

"Nah that's it." She answered.

"Eight twenty-three."

"*Eight twenty-three?* Goddamn!" Yolanda growled as she reached into her back pocket to retrieve her wallet. "Da fuck. That shit better come with a happy meal toy or something."

The cashier turned back around to fill up more orders. "Filet o'fish meal with an apple pie!" She called out. Yolanda held out a twenty, but the cashier kept moving to fill more orders. She filled up another bag and then looked at the receipt stuck to it.

Yolanda thought she was coming to take her payment but she proceeded to walk past towards the ice cream machine. There, she whipped up a dessert for someone before returning to the counter. "One super-sized big mac meal, grilled chicken salad, and Oreo McFlurry!" Another anxious customer squeezed next to Yolanda to claim their order.

"Aye-o! You gon' let me pay for this food or what?" She asked.

Once again, the cashier sucked her teeth, placed her hand on her hip, and walked back to her register to take Yolanda's money. "Out of twenty," she mumbled with a sigh. She punched in more stuff on her screen. Then the cash drawer popped open.

Before she could count out the change, Yolanda interrupted. "Wait! I changed my mind. Scratch that. I want a quarter pounder instead."

"Are you serious?" The cashier asked with an attitude.

"Do I look like I'm playing?"

"Well they're not the same price." The cashier replied.

"Okay, well whatever. What's the difference?"

The cashier looked at her screen, then looked up at the menu, and back to her screen. "Susanna!" She yelled.

"What's the problem?" Yolanda asked.

"There is no problem."

"Well how much is it?" She asked again.

"Hold on. I'll tell you in a minute." With that, she went back to filling orders. People in the line behind Yolanda began huffing and puffing in annoyance.

"What the fuck y'all looking at? It's like five other lines in here!" She hurled at the other customers who said nothing in response.

Susanna, who appeared to be the manager, walked over from another register a few lines down. "Amiyah, what's up?"

"I need you to back something out for me."

"Why? What is it?" She questioned.

"She don't know what she wants." That was the wrong thing for Amiyah to say.

"Um I know what the fuck I want! I just told you, but for

whatever reason you can't seem to tell me how much it is." Amiyah just looked in response, clearly trying to hold her tongue.

"Okay. Okay. Let me just clear this out. Then I will take your order." Susanna said, trying to calm Yolanda. She tapped the screen some more and slid a key into the register to complete the transaction. "Okay, what would you like?" Yolanda repeated her order for Susanna. "Is there anything else?"

"No."

"Okay. Eight fifty-six, please." Susanna said. Yolanda handed her the twenty and Susanna gave her the change before returning to her own register.

"How hard was that?" She hissed at Amiyah.

Amiyah mumbled under her breath as she turned to fill up more orders, "Dike bitch."

"What the fuck you say? Come over here and say that to my face!"

"Whatever, ain't nobody got time to argue with you." Amiyah replied as she stood near the food belt waiting for the order.

"Yeah that's exactly what I thought. Stay back there smelling like french fry grease wit'cho minimum wage-making ass. You a cashier and can't even subtract to figure out a thirty-three-cent difference. Dumb ass! Silly ass bitch! You better stay in school!"

Amiyah had had enough. "Look I don't know who you think you talking to but you better fall back. I'm not the one. That lesbian *think I got a penis so I'ma act like a dude* shit don't scare me. I might make minimum wage but at least I don't look like a fucking linebacker you ugly ass bitch."

"Who you calling a bitch? You obviously don't know who I am!"

"I look like I give a damn who you are? You better hope I don't have my homie in the back spit in your shit." She threatened.

"Yeah aight. You better be careful who you talking to. Don't let your slick mouth get you fucked up in here. I'm sure you don't wanna get that ass beat in front of all of Mickey D's."

Amiyah couldn't be happier to see Yolanda's food arrive on the belt. By this time Susanna was back on the scene attempting to diffuse the situation. "Hey hey. I told you before, Amiyah. That's not how we work here. That's not how we do customer service. Now just give the lady her food."

Amiyah grabbed Yolanda's fries and tossed them in the bag. Then she nearly threw the bag onto the counter. "Next in line!" she fumed.

"I – I know you ain't just throw my shit. You shouldn't have done that."

Amiyah ignored her and continued taking the next man's order. Yolanda turned and headed towards the exit through the crowd. Amiyah mumbled under her breath, "That's what I thought. Ain't gon' do shit." It wasn't clear if Yolanda heard her or not, but either way she already had plans of her own.

No more than two minutes passed before Yolanda appeared out of nowhere behind the counter. "Now what's that shit you was talkin'?"

Amiyah never saw the tray coming for her face as she turned around. All that was heard was the *crunch* of her nose against the back of the tray. She immediately grabbed the throbbing cartilage as it began to quickly leak blood onto her uniform. Yolanda wasn't done. In the blink of an eye she came full force with the tray two more times, busting Amiyah's lip, and slamming it into her already broken nose again. Yolanda threw the tray down and two other nearby employees attempted to pull her off of the girl, but they were no match. Flinging them both to the side like a raging bull, all she saw was red. She grabbed the bloody cashier with both hands by the neck then kneed her in her stomach. Once she was doubled over in pain, Yolanda pushed her down to the floor where she proceeded to kick her in the ribs and stomp on her face.

"What are you doing! Stop! Stop!" Susanna screamed but to no avail. "I'm calling the police!"

Beaten and bloody, that still wasn't enough for Yolanda. "What's up now, bitch? I don't hear you saying shit!" She slapped her across the face with an open palm. "*That's* for making me wait in line so long!" She punched her in the jaw. "*That's* for all that attitude you gave me!" Then she grabbed the girl by her hair at the roots, wrapping it around her hand once before dragging her across the floor. "And this ..." She stopped in front of the fry station, grabbed one of the baskets that sat in the hot grease, and dumped the fries onto the floor. "*This* is for all that shit you was talkin'!" She held the hot fry basket to the side of Amiyah's face and let it rest there, branding the girl's cheek. Amiyah kicked and screamed in a futile attempt to escape Yolanda's hold. When Yolanda lifted the fry basket from her face, it left a rather large and vivid grid pattern in its place.

Satisfied with her release of rage, Yolanda hissed, "Now ... say something." She waited only for a short moment then released her grip on the girl's hair and shoved her to the side. "That's exactly what I thought." She looked around at all the scared, staring, faces and smirked. "And I'm taking these 'cause my fries were cold." She grabbed a large sac of french fries, then hopped over the counter and attempted to make her exit, but the police met her at the door. "Don't worry. No need to cuff me, officers. My work here is done. I'll go peacefully. I just wanna eat my fries."

***

"Yolanda, I can't keep bailing you out of these same situations." Dr. Grigsby whispered as she walked briskly out the door of the police station.

"Look, you know I'll pay you for the inconvenience, Doc."

"It's not about the money. You have to learn to control your anger. How many times do you think the judge is going to let you off on your own recognizance? Not to mention, the damage you did to that poor girl's face." The doctor scolded.

"That lil' bitch deserved it."

Dr. Grigsby stopped in her tracks. "Look, I can't keep coming to your rescue every time you get in trouble. It falls outside our patient – client boundaries, Yolanda."

"Fuck it. I don't need you." She spat. A man walking past

towards the station stared. "Da fuck you lookin' at baldy?"

"See, that's what I'm talking about. There's just no reason for that." The man, unsure of how to respond, continued to stare but quickened his pace for the door. "And it's only because of me and the strings I was able to pull *yet again* that you're on this side of the door right now. It would be nice if you showed at least a little bit of gratitude."

"Yeah whatever. What? I'm supposed to be kissing your ass just because you think you're my savior or something?" The doctor, at a loss for words, just shook her head in disbelief. "We still gon' have our session or what, Doc?" Yolanda asked, changing the subject.

Once back in the doctor's home office, Yolanda plopped herself across the couch and closed her eyes.

"I think we should talk about what happened today." Dr. Grigsby began. Yolanda sighed and rolled her eyes. "You don't want to talk about it?"

"There's really nothing to tell. The bitch got smart so I handled that ass. Case closed." She shrugged and placed the back of her hand on her forehead.

"We have to get you more used to using your words, Yolanda. That's what the point of all this is. Now ... take me step by step. What happened?" She asked softly.

"All I wanted to do was pop into Micky D's to get something quick before I came to our session." She started.

"Okay."

"I don't know why that place always has to be so damned packed, people stepping all over you and whatnot. I hate it."

"So, if you know you hate it, why did you go in there?" The doctor questioned.

"I just told you; to grab something to eat right quick."

"Okay, so you're in McDonalds. What happens next?"

"First, I got the dude behind me stepping on my feet, fucking up my boots. You know I keep my shits clean, Doc." She said.

"So, is that what upset you? You were mad because the man stepped on your boots?"

"Nah – I mean yeah! Well, no, it wasn't just that. We got all these foreigners coming over here, taking all the jobs, and making everything so crowded. It just makes me feel like a sardine in a can. You know?" She paused for the doctor's acknowledgement.

"Well, you know Yolanda, a lot of these immigrants come here seeking better opportunities for themselves and their families. A lot of them come from very poor, poverty-stricken places and they just want a better life. Can you understand that?"

"Yeah, I get all that, Doc. But it's still just too many of 'em. But I don't even think that's what set me off."

"Okay then let's get to it. What do you think it was that *did* set you off?" Dr. Grigsby asked.

"I don't know exactly. It was just like all those people were in there staring at me. Then I get to the counter and the silly broad has an attitude with me for no reason, talkin' smart n' shit. Then she's helpin' everybody else and actin' like I'm not even standin' there. Then she called me a dike and talkin' all this other garbage. I just felt..." Yolanda paused as she tried to search for the right words to describe her feelings.

"Felt what, Yolanda?"

"I don't know. I just felt ... disrespected. I felt like I didn't matter, like she was takin' me for a joke or somethin', and it pissed me off."

"Okay this is good. You didn't know her, right? So why did it matter so much to you that she didn't take you seriously?"

"I don't know. Because..." Yolanda searched her brain for an answer.

"I know the last time we talked about your parents you shared with me how devastating their separation was before they finally got divorced and your dad left you."

"Yeah *and*? Why y'all shrinks always try'na tie something back to the parents. What do daddy issues have to do wit' a hoe gettin' smart with me at Mickey D's?" Yolanda winced in annoyance.

"It's not about daddy issues. When we talked about your parents you mentioned that they never discussed the divorce or the separation with you."

"They didn't. All they cared about was themselves."

"And this made you angry." The doctor stated the question as a suggestion.

"Of course, pissed me off!"

"Do you see where I'm going with this?"

"Not really, Doc." Yolanda confessed.

"It seems like you get angry whenever you feel overlooked or ignored. When your parents separated they didn't talk to you about it. They didn't ask you how it made you feel. You had no say whatsoever in the decision."

"Yeah, that's right." She cosigned.

"It was the same with the young lady at McDonald's today. You felt overlooked and your feelings weren't taken into consideration. This set you off." Yolanda, connecting the dots, didn't respond. "Yolanda, how have the anger management sessions been going?"

"Ugh! Alright, I guess ... The truth is I can't stand them."

"Oh? Why is that?"

"I don't like group therapy. All they do there is bitch and complain over stupid stuff. *'My husband ate the last piece of pie and it made me upset' 'This lady at the gym called me fat and I got so pissed'* They get mad over the dumbest things. They don't have *real* problems. They're just a bunch of spoiled ass adults who throw childish temper tantrums when they don't get their way." She explained.

The doctor couldn't hold in her chuckle. "Did someone really get mad over a piece of pie?"

"Yeah. Dumb, right?" Yolanda shook her head.

"Okay, well, aside from the people, have you learned any useful techniques? Ways to help you control your anger?"

"I don't know." Yolanda paused. Then a light bulb went off in her head. "Oh! I've been going to the gym."

"The gym?" The doctor questioned.

"Yeah. My homie got a lil' gym around the way where he teaches boxing. One of the anger management techniques was to take up some type of physical activity. You know, to redirect the anger. When I get in there with that bag, I just go in. That helps a little."

"Good. I'm so glad to hear that. That's great progress, Yolanda." Dr. Grigsby said enthusiastically.

"Yeah ... I guess." Yolanda let a tiny smirk tug at the corner of her mouth in pride. "I start sparring in a couple of weeks. That should be even better. Then I get to take my anger out on a real live person."

"Uh oh. Just don't do to them what you did to that poor girl today." The doctor cautioned.

Yolanda snickered, "I'll try not to."

"Seriously, Yolanda. You're still on probation and you don't need to give the courts any reason to rethink their decision."

Yolanda had been in and out of jail her entire teen life straight into adulthood. Her biggest charge was arson and she came very close to serving serious time for it. She was only sixteen when she'd set her former best friend's car on fire after finding out she'd stolen Yolanda's girlfriend of the time. Being so young worked in her favor. The judge let her off with a slap on the wrist since she was a minor and no one was hurt. Even though she was only given three years of probation, Yolanda always found a way to violate that probation, extending the time period even longer each time.

"I know, Dr. Grigsby. I know."

5 BHAVNA & CHRISTOPHER

Bhavna lost track of time as she stood in the cereal aisle of the partially empty supermarket. After showing up for her shift at Duane Reed that day, the pharmacy's confused manager said Bhavna wasn't supposed to be there. There must've been a mix up with scheduling; so, she was sent home at noon. Now she took her time grocery shopping. She knew there wasn't much they really needed, but wasn't ready to go home. The grocery store was a distraction. *If you keep yourself busy, you won't have time to think about sex so much. Stay productive, Bhavna.* She heard the doctor's voice play in her head. "Stay productive, Bhavna." She whispered out loud to herself.

She'd gone down the aisle to pick out cereal for Ashok and the kids. She already tossed a box of Captain Crunch in the shopping cart for Nirav and Zobia. Now she stared at shelves of flakes; corn flakes, whole wheat flakes, multi grain flakes, frosted flakes. The distraction wasn't working. All she could think of was her encounters with Stephen. God, they were amazing. She felt her skin warm and began to softly rub her neck beneath the collar of her pharmacy lab coat.

"I always liked Lucky Charms, myself." The sudden booming voice startled her and she clutched the collar close around her neck.

Embarrassed, she chuckled. "Oh, I guess I started daydreaming again. I'm sorry." She smiled bashfully as she stepped to the side.

"No need to apologize. I saw a damsel in a cereal distress and what kind of gentleman would I be if I didn't come to her rescue?" Bhavna laughed nervously. "I'm Christopher, by the way."

"My name is Bhavna."

"It's a pleasure to meet you, Bhavna."

His voice was charismatic, but he didn't need to say another word. His scent alone already had Bhavna pulsating inside of her polyester slacks. "Yes, nice to meet you too, Christopher." She tried to scurry off.

"Bhavna, you seem familiar. Have we met before?" He asked.

"No, I don't think so."

"Are you a doctor or something?"

She looked down at her lab coat then answered, "No, I'm a pharmacist – at Duane Reed."

"That must be it!"

Bhavna smiled and nodded in response. She could feel her urges growing stronger by the second. It didn't matter that she didn't know Christopher. He could've been anyone. He could've been the frail young cashier, the balding, pot-bellied, stock boy – anyone. Her body didn't seem to care that she was in a public grocery store. She could feel her nipples begin to pierce the T-shirt she wore under the lab coat.

"Are you okay?" He asked.

"Yes. Yes, I'm fine."

An old woman hunched over a shopping cart made her way down the aisle. She stopped to eye a box of Life before continuing.

"Are you sure? You're flushed." Christopher insisted. The old woman paused and looked at Bhavna as if she was going to say something, but decided against it, then turned the corner at the end of the aisle.

"It is a little warm in here. I just need to get some air. That's all."

"Come. Maybe a little splash of water on your face will help. The bathroom's back here." He led the way through the cloudy plastic pains separating the store from the warehouse without giving Bhavna a chance to object.

She stood hunched over the sink in the unisex bathroom in the rear of the store. The coolness crashed against her face as she took a deep breath in, eyes closed. She reached for a paper towel, then stood up straight and dabbed at her face. When her eyes opened she was startled to see Christopher in the mirror's reflection.

"I hope I didn't frighten you. I just wanted to make sure you were okay." He said.

Bhavna didn't respond. Instead, the two stood staring into each other's eyes through the reflection in the mirror. Christopher carefully and slowly removed Bhavna's lab coat from her shoulders and neatly hung it on the hook on the back of the door. Bhavna closed her eyes and waited. She felt his strong hands start at her shoulders then work their way down to cup her breasts, firmly massaging them in full circles. Her chest heaved in and out as her breath deepened. She could feel herself getting lost in Christopher's touch.

This was insane, dangerous, she knew, but her body betrayed her. Bhavna felt a sudden tug on her hair, causing her neck to bend to the side. The feel of Christopher's lips against the thin area of skin rendered her helpless against the pleasures to come. Her eyes stayed sealed shut and only fluttered in response to the sensation of Christopher's teeth sinking into her neck. The sudden sting of pain sent an electric shock straight to Bhavna's center as she felt herself moisten.

"We should get you out of these." Her eyes popped open to find Christopher's hands moving swiftly to yank down her slacks so that they clung to her knees. Suddenly she felt embarrassed with her plain cotton bloomers on display. There was nothing sexy about the lime green and navy-blue striped undergarment. Usually when she knew she'd be on the prowl, she'd wear something from her stash of sexy panties or thongs made of slinky materials like lace, silk or satin. Christopher didn't seem to mind, though. He gently slid them down to sit atop the halted slacks.

"Turn around." He instructed. Bhavna did as told. Too disgusted with herself to face the stranger, she closed her eyes again. She let her body lead her. Firmly, she planted her palms on the edge of the sink and hoisted herself up. The cool surface felt good against her bottom in contrast to the fire running through the rest of her body. Christopher grabbed the middle of Bhavna's pants by the crotch and slowly began to raise her legs straight up to the ceiling, exposing all of her womanhood. He grabbed Bhavna's wrist and guided it to her ankles where she grabbed a hold, careful to steady herself on the edge of the sink. Christopher dropped to his knees on the grungy tiled floor and began his work.

Bhavna moaned in ecstasy with every flick of Christopher's tongue. Gripping her by the hips, he moved fast. She gyrated her hips in rhythm until she felt her first climax coming. Her body jerked with her back arching to its limit. Three more orgasms followed, each one just as strong as the first. She shook involuntarily until every last drop of her wetness had been squeezed out like an orange being juiced.

Satisfied with his work, Christopher stood up slowly without a word and wiped the corners of his mouth with the back of his hand. Bhavna stayed perched on the edge of the sink, her legs grounded back on the floor, her eyes still shut. Her chest puffed in and out as she regained control of her breath. No more words were exchanged. There was nothing left to say. The deed was done. Now that the pleasure faded, shame rushed into Bhavna. She didn't have to tell Christopher. He just knew. He felt it and, with that, he took his cue to leave. She didn't hear the door open or close but she could sense that he was gone. She cracked her eyelids to find that he had, in fact, disappeared just as swiftly as he'd appeared.

6 DR. GRIGSBY'S CLIENTS

"Helen! Helen, wake up!" Claude stood over his bed, shaking Dr. Grigsby by the shoulders. His OCD didn't allow for them to share a bed just yet. His bedroom was set up like a hotel room with two full-size beds set side by side. Whenever Dr. Grigsby slept over she occupied one – the one closest the window. He occupied the other closest to the door. He needed to be closest to the exit. Otherwise, he couldn't sleep.

This night, Dr. Grigsby couldn't sleep either. She tossed and turned all night long. She'd started off talking and moaning into the quiet of the night, then ended up screaming. Claude noticed that his girlfriend did seem a bit preoccupied earlier that evening, but he didn't pry.

"Helen! Helen, honey, please wake up!" He lightly patted her face so as to slap her out of it without having to actually slap her.

Dr. Grigsby swung her fists wildly through the air before shooting bolt upright in the bed. "Wha-what?" Her heart raced and black synthetic strands of hair stuck to her face, drenched in sweat.

"Just breathe. Breathe." Claude coached as he tried to ease her loud, exaggerated, gasps for air. "You're okay now. You're okay, sweetie."

"Oh my god. What happened?"

"Here, just relax. I'll get you a glass of water." Claude propped up two pillows to support her back. He made his way to the attached bathroom where he filled a glass with cool water from the tap. He returned and sat on the bed next to Dr. Grigsby, "Here, take a sip."

Dr. Grigsby did as told. "I'm so sorry, Claude. I must've had a nightmare. I didn't mean to scare you."

"It's okay. I figured as much…Who is Yolanda?"

"Yolanda?"

"Yeah, you kept yelling *'Yolanda, no! Please don't, Yolanda!'*"

Dr. Grigsby took another gulp of water before responding, "I don't know who that is."

"You don't?"

"No. You know how dreams are. A lot of times they make no sense." She didn't want to discuss her patients with Claude. She didn't want him knowing what she had to deal with on a regular basis. She was afraid it might scare him off.

"I think it's your nerves."

"My nerves?"

"Yes. I think you're just nervous about meeting my family this weekend, and that's why you're having nightmares."

"Well, maybe."

Claude took her hand, "You have nothing to be nervous about. They're going to love you just as much as I do."

Dr. Grigsby smiled and squeezed his hand in response, before he quickly snatched it back, rubbing it over his pajama bottoms. She tried to appear at ease, but the visions of Yolanda wielding the container of gasoline was so vivid in her mind. This wasn't the first time she dreamt about one of her patients. Though the dreams were always slightly different each time, and they always came in bits and pieces. Sometimes she'd see Christopher with a fiery rage blazing in his eyes, his stare unflinching and evil. Other times it was Jessica's hands squeezing the delicate neck of a faceless child. This time there was a huge fire. Orange flames leapt everywhere. There was a car and she could see the seared, melting flesh of someone trapped inside pressed up against the window as they tried to claw their way out.

Dr. Grigsby took a gulp of the water, then squeezed her eyes shut. She inhaled before opening them. The truth was she was excited to meet Claude's family. She never managed to maintain any romantic relationship long enough to meet a boyfriend's family. Claude's Obsessive-Compulsive Disorder kept him from having too many girlfriends. This was a big move for them both. She tried hard to force the images from her head and restore the excitement.

***

It was a dreary Friday, the day before Dr. Grigsby was to take the drive Upstate with Claude to meet his family. It was also her first time hosting a group therapy session for her patients. She felt rattled as she rushed about, mumbling to herself, as she set up chairs in a small circle in her office. She pushed her chaise back against the wall. It would be a tight squeeze, but it would work, she thought. Dr. Planthers suggested that maybe it was time for Dr. Grigsby's patients to all meet one another, and even offered to sit in on the session. With the exception of Yolanda, they were all suffering from issues related to addiction. Though each addiction varied – Christopher's addiction to the high that robbing brought, Jessica's addiction to attention and narcotics, and Bhavna's addiction to orgasm. Even though Yolanda didn't show any signs of addiction to anything, both doctors agreed that perhaps she could benefit from the actual social interaction by learning to be around others who were not like her.

Jessica was the first to arrive. Dr. Grigsby could sense that she was anxious by her insistent knuckle cracking. "Is something wrong, Jessica?" She asked as they took a seat in the circle.

"I don't know. I don't really want to meet with the other patients. I like it when it's just you and me, Dr. Grigsby." The teen confessed while shooting Dr. Planthers a quick glance. Dr. Planthers sat in a poorly lit corner outside of the circle, her small notepad out and ready to scribble on.

"I know this will be a little different from our usual meetings, but let's just give it a chance. Okay?"

"Why?" Jessica questioned.

"I think you'll be surprised to see how talking to others who are also struggling with things can be helpful to you."

"I really don't see how." She argued, sitting with her arms crossed.

"How about we make a deal?" Dr. Grigsby suggested.

"What kind of deal? I sure could use some cash."

Dr. Grigsby chuckled. "Nothing like that, Jessica. Give group therapy a try for me just this one time. If you really hate it, you don't have to come back again. We'll just go back to one-on-one therapy. How's that?"

"That's it? That's your deal?" Jessica wasn't impressed. Dr. Grigsby nodded. "Fine. Whatever."

Yolanda and Bhavna arrived at the same time. Bhavna was quiet, timid. She and Dr. Grigsby had discussed the group therapy beforehand, its goal and what to expect. Yolanda looked angry, but that was normal for her.

She plopped down and folded her arms across her black puffy vest. Each black Timberland boot met the floor with an exaggerated thud. Then she slid her butt forward and leaned back so that she sat slouched in the chair. Similar to Jessica, her reluctance to being there showed.

"What's this all about, Doc?" She asked in a huff.

"Welcome, Yolanda. It's always nice to see you." Dr. Grigsby sarcastically lied. "This is Jessica and Bhavna. Ladies, this is Yolanda. I was just explaining to Jessica why I wanted us all to meet tonight."

"Well?" Yolanda waited for an explanation.

"I think one thing that lacks in our one-on-one sessions is my ability to relate to your individual issues."

"Oh, so you think you better than us?" Yolanda was defensive.

"No. No, that's not what I'm saying, Yolanda. I just mean sometimes it's easier to talk to someone who is dealing with similar circumstances. Someone who understands what you're facing."

"Oh, so you mean I should talk to someone else who understands what it's like to wanna chin check a bitch when she gets out of pocket. I already have the anger management sessions for that."

"No, not exa —"

"And who's she?" Yolanda cut Dr. Grigsby off before she had a chance to explain.

Dr. Grigsby took a deep breath, and prepared to respond, but Dr. Planthers answered. "I'm Dr. Planthers. I'm a … *friend* of Dr. Grigsby's and I'm just here to observe. So, don't mind me. Just act as though I'm not even here!"

The room grew quiet, and everyone stared at Dr. Planthers. Then, all of a sudden, a voice boomed. "It's okay everybody! I'm here now!" Christopher showed nothing but teeth across his face.

"Hi Christopher," Dr. Grigsby's greeting was bland and dry. "Everyone, this is Christopher."

"Whooo hooo! Looks like I'm late to the party. Hope I didn't miss anything, ladies." He took a slow scan around the room while licking his lips like a dog in heat. He did a double take when his eyes fell on Bhavna. His grin widened and he gave a wink. "Nice to see *you*."

Bhavna blushed and looked into her lap. Once again, her body reacted against her will. She felt a fever coming on and an increase in her heart rate. She pulsated between her legs. Dr. Planthers noticed her discomfort and jotted something quickly. The scratchy sound of her pencil against the pad drew Christopher's attention. He felt that same peculiar feeling he'd felt the last time he saw Dr. Planthers, like he knew her from somewhere. He recalled their awkward encounter at the end of his last one-on-one session as he left Dr. Grigsby's office.

Dr. Planthers had been waiting for Christopher to arrive. She didn't let on to Dr. Grigsby, but that was where her main interest lie. She smiled kindly, "Hi Christopher. I'm Dr. Planthers. I was just telling the others I'm just here to observe your session."

"*Observe?* What are we? Fish in a bowl?" Something about Dr. Planthers' presence made Christopher uneasy. He didn't trust the bitch.

"Okay, Christopher. If you don't mind, I'd like to get started." Dr. Grigsby said, wearily. Treating Christopher drained her energy. He had such a big and demanding personality. Even as boisterous as Yolanda could be, Christopher was a master manipulator who required much more dissecting and commanded much more attention. She began to wonder if having him participate in the group therapy was a mistake. It would require him to share her attention with others, something he wasn't accustomed to.

Christopher waved his hand and bowed his head, "By all means. Please. Don't get your panties in a bunch, Dr. Grigsby." Jessica snickered, which only fed Christopher's already inflated ego. Dr. Grigsby's cheeks warmed and Dr. Planters made additional notes.

"Okay, then…" Dr. Grigsby started by asking each of the patients to express why they thought they were in therapy, what they viewed as their biggest challenge and what their greatest fears were. Bhavna's greatest fear was losing her children, Nirav and Zobia. Yolanda and Christopher both claimed they weren't afraid of anything; while Jessica only admitted to her issue with drugs. It was clear that she was still in denial about her Munchausen Syndrome. When Dr. Grigsby pressed her about it, Jessica only became defensive. "But what about the children you hurt?" She'd asked.

"Oh shit! You're a baby diddler?" Christopher provoked.

"No!"

"That's fucked up! I've done a lot of shit in my life, but you messin' with kids? I should stomp the shit outta you right now!" Yolanda's anger rose in her chest.

"Now just hold on a minute! Yolanda, remember where we are. We're not here to judge Jessica. We're here to help each other." Dr. Grigsby grew nervous but tried to keep control of the situation.

"Fuck that!" Yolanda thrusted one closed fist into the open

palm of her other hand.

"I'm not a baby diddler!" Jessica yelled out in protest. "Please! Please don't hit me." She cowered. "I-I didn't…*touch* them – well not like *that*."

"What the hell does that mean?" Christopher amusingly asked with a smirk smeared across his lips.

"Let's all take a deep breath. Jessica, why don't you explain?" Dr. Grigsby suggested. Bhavna, though quiet, felt a burning disgust growing within that took form of bile rising in the back of her throat. "And we're all going to listen. Remember. That's what this group is about – *listening* and using our words." Dr. Grigsby coached. "Go on."

"Like I was trying to say, I didn't touch them like *molest* them, if that's what you think." She swallowed before continuing, "I just…I just…"

"Well? Just what?" Yolanda demanded to know.

"God! You are killing me with boredom, little girl. Will you just spit it out already?" Christopher complained. Dr. Planthers worked her pencil over the small pages of her notepad with ferocity. The more she wrote, the more it annoyed Christopher because it seemed as though her pencil moved the most whenever his mouth was open. "And what the hell are you writing over there?" Dr. Planthers paused and offered a manufactured smile but didn't speak.

"Can we please let Jessica speak? Please!" Dr. Grigsby pleaded. The room fell quiet again. "Jessica, I've told you before. Therapy will only help if you're completely honest. Go ahead. Tell us what you mean…about you and the children."

"I – sometimes when I babysit kids, you know for my neighbors and stuff…sometimes I – sometimes they ended up having to go to the hospital." She blurted out the last part quickly as her voice shook.

"Go to the hospital for what?" Bhavna broke her silence.

"Because they couldn't breathe."

"What do you mean *'they couldn't breathe'*? Why couldn't they breathe?" Yolanda's voice never softened.

"I don't know. I –"

"Jessica," Dr. Grigsby chastised.

"I mean because I put a pillow over their faces. I…" Jessica's eyes welled. Her voice cracked and she couldn't finish.

"You *suffocated* the kids?" Yolanda asked in disbelief. Jessica gave a short but emphatic nod.

"Holy shit. You're not a baby diddler. You're a kid killer!" It was the first time Christopher, too, appeared disgusted.

"No! I didn't kill anyone. I saved them!" Jessica protested.

"Saved them from who? Yourself?" Christopher patronized. "You tried to smother poor little kids and you're trying to call yourself a hero? Wow, I thought I was screwed up in the head." His voice rose with each tongue lashing.

"And what about you?" Dr. Grigsby dared to challenge Christopher on his actions.

"What about me?" He responded. He waited for Dr. Grigsby's response but the constant scratching of Dr. Planthers' pencil ate away at his nerves. His paranoia was getting the best of him. Why was she really there? Why had Dr. Grigsby allowed her there?

"What about the violent things you've done? You've hurt people too, Christopher." Dr. Grigsby tried to speak calmly. She knew this was a trigger point.

Christopher's nostrils flared and his eyes glared. "I don't want to talk about that!"

"Nah, fuck that! If everybody else gotta share, so do you!" Yolanda pressed with attitude. "You ain't special."

"Why don't you just shut your face!" Christopher spat. Through his state of vehemence, he noticed Dr. Planthers nervously dig through her purse to retrieve her cell phone. Her hand trembled as she began to press buttons, and it set him off. "What the hell are you doing with that phone? Have you been recording us? Who are you calling? Are you calling the police?" He lurched forward from the chair, causing it to topple backwards onto the floor.

"No. No – I. Helen." Dr. Planthers looked frightened as she stared up into Christopher's pupils.

"What are you calling Dr. Grigsby for? She can't help you

now. What do you think you're doing? Give me this!" Christopher snatched the phone from Dr. Planthers' hand, then hurled it against the back wall with such force it cracked before hitting the floor.

"Helen! Helen!" Dr. Planthers' voice shook as she begged for Dr. Grigsby to call some order to the session.

"Christopher! You need to calm down right now!" Dr. Grigsby ordered, but he stormed off through the door instead. The session ended with Christopher's departure.

***

"Are you sure you're feeling okay, sweetie?" Claude asked, briefly glancing at Dr. Grigsby, but never allowing his hands to slip from their positions on the steering wheel. He was a stiff flap of cardboard and looked uncomfortable driving. He'd spent fifteen minutes adjusting the mirrors to their precise positions before getting on the road, and every few minutes he'd glance up into the rearview mirror. He kept the pressure of his foot just so on the accelerator to maintain a consistent speed of sixty-four as they made their way up Route 87.

Dr. Grigsby smiled, "Yes, I already told you. I'm fine, Claude."

"Okay." He returned the smile. With the radio turned off, because Claude didn't like any distractions while driving, the short, repeated, spurts of a vibrating cell phone could be heard. Dr. Grigsby took out the phone, looked at it for a moment before deciding to send the call to voicemail. "Was that Dr. Planthers?"

Dr. Grigsby sighed. She was on edge and annoyed that Dr. Planthers was calling again and that Claude asked about it again. "Yes."

"How come you don't answer? It might be important if she's calling again." Dr. Planthers hadn't spoken to Dr. Grigsby since the session the evening before.

"It's not."

"How do you know if you don't answer?" Claude insisted.

"She's just calling to talk about one of my patients. I told you the group session didn't go so well yesterday. It can wait until we get back."

It was Claude's turn to sigh, "okay".

The road was clear. It was the afternoon and, even though the sun shined brightly, it was only sixteen degrees outside. The tree branches were frosty with ice from the rain the night before and the pavement wore an ashy white film. Ice covered the massive rock forms that aligned the highway. For reasons she couldn't explain, Dr. Grigsby felt an increasing anxiety growing roots in her chest. The further they drove, the deeper the roots expanded, their reach multiplying to travel the length of her body. She had an unsettling feeling as though she'd been this way before, seen these big boulders, saw the sign for Poughkeepsie before, but couldn't remember. For reasons unexplained she felt unsafe.

It wasn't until they pulled into the semicircle driveway of Claude's parents' home that she began to feel at ease again. She knew for sure she hadn't been here before. The grandiose house boasted the wealth of Claude's family. The brick driveway placed them directly in front of the double French doors that led into a two-story foyer.

Mrs. Langdon met them at the door. "Please, please come in. Let's get you two out of that cold." The white-haired tiny woman smiled widely as she rubbed her own arms, her slate-grey eyes lit with excitement. "You must be Helen." Without hesitation, she scooped Dr. Grigsby into her thin arms for a warm embrace.

"Hi, Mrs. Langdon. It's so nice to meet you." Dr. Grigsby spoke into her shoulder. She sensed a genuine warmth radiate from Claude's mother, and she decided she liked her already.

"Mom, she can't breathe," Claude laughed lightly.

"Oh, you're next, mister." Mrs. Langdon planted her lips on Claude's cheek and gave him a squeeze. She was one of the few people that was able to get this close to Claude. "Let me take this." She offered a hand as Dr. Grigsby shimmied out of her down coat. "Here, put these away." She instructed Claude towards the coat closet nearby, then she took Dr. Grigsby by the hand. "Come on. Everybody's in the family room."

They crossed a white marble floor with black swirls, passing a baby grand piano on the way. As they made their way down a short hall, Dr. Grigsby glanced at family photos that included a younger Claude when he had more hair.

"Everybody! Claude and his girlfriend, Helen, are here. Helen, this is everybody." She exclaimed, still wearing the same friendly smile. Everyone sat around a burning fireplace, watching a TV that was mounted just above. She introduced Dr. Grigsby to Claude's younger sister, Sarah, her husband, Brian, and their ten and eight-year olds, Mandy and Ben. Claude's father sat closest to the fire in a brown leather recliner with his feet kicked up on the coffee table and a drink in his hand. He was Claude, only thirty or so years older, with a few more wrinkles and a much bigger belly. "We're just waiting on Davie and then we'll eat." Mrs. Langdon informed. Davie was Claude's older brother. "Have a seat. Can I get you anything? Some water? Juice? Tea?"

"Sure, I'll have a glass of orange juice if you have it." Dr. Grigsby said.

"You got it, hon." Mrs. Langdon flitted off just as Claude entered.

"Uncle Claude! Uncle Claude!" Ben and Mandy yelped as they rushed Claude's midsection, knocking him off balance momentarily. Though happy to see his niece and nephew, his flaming cheeks gave innuendo to his nervousness from the touch of little fingers.

"Hey! Heyyyy!" After a pinch of a cheek and the pat of a head, Claude was rescued.

"Okay, give your uncle some room, kids." Brian instructed. "How's it going, Claude? Good to see you, brother-in-law." He stood and leaned between his children's heads to shake Claude's hand, conscious not to linger for too long. Claude appreciated Brian's understanding of his lifelong condition, but that didn't stop him from whipping out his handkerchief to wipe his palms that had begun to sweat. Brian took no offense and reclaimed his seat on the sofa. Sarah and Mr. Langdon kept their distance but said their hellos.

The group chatted up Dr. Grigsby as they waited for Davie to arrive. She felt at ease around these people, and was glad she'd finally come to meet Claude's family. She knew how close Claude was to them, especially Mrs. Langdon. Claude told her how it was she who maintained her patience with him over the years. She was the one to take him to all of his therapy appointments. Mr. Langdon would sometimes lose his temper with his boy who refused to swing a bat that other boys had held and swung moments before him. Even once he had his own personal bat, the precise thirty-three practice swings that had to happen before Claude was ready drove Mr. Langdon nuts. Not to mention the embarrassment he felt when Claude freaked out, shrieking in terror underneath his first tackle on the football field – those bodies, *dirty* bodies, piled on top of him with their sweat and germs smearing against his exposed arms and shins.

Though Sarah loved both of her big brothers, Claude's ongoing behavior, and her parents' never-ending focus on fixing it, did suck up any attention that might have been left over for the only girl in the family. She had to learn to make a serious effort to ward off the resentment, and this she had so humbly conquered. She grew to look up to Claude over the years. He was her go-to whenever she was stumped on an algebra assignment or needed help researching a science project. And, in his own way, Claude learned to play with his little sister from a distance. Board games and puzzles became essential to their interaction.

When Davie arrived, it was clear that he was the golden boy of the family. Where Claude disappointed, Davie picked up the slack in the sports arena. The Langdon's kept a small room dedicated to his numerous football, track and basketball trophies. His athletic abilities led him to a full scholarship to Columbia University where his popularity only blossomed. Even though they didn't share much in common, it didn't stop Davie from taking his little brother under his wing when he'd arrived at the University two years after him. Davie's rippled physique, pouty red lips and inherited grey eyes made his life with the ladies all the easier. The fact that his confidence bordered ever so slightly on an almost unnoticeable arrogance translated to sexiness amongst his female peers. As much as Davie tried to share his good fortune, Claude was just too awkward to ever get acclimated with the ladies. Still, Davie's efforts in including him never ceased.

It was only upon Davie's arrival that Dr. Grigsby's slight pulse of anxiety began to beat again. It was the way Davie took a step back and squinted at her when Claude introduced the two that caused her to divert her eyes. "I feel like I've seen you somewhere before," he'd said.

"Oh no you don't. You can have any lady you'd like, but this one's taken." Claude proudly teased. "Save your cheesy lines for those ladies around your job." Everyone except Dr. Grigsby laughed it off.

Mrs. Langdon wasn't the best cook, but Dr. Grigsby was a great actress and, apparently, so was the rest of the family. Perhaps they'd all grown use to the bland baked chicken cutlets, peppery green beans and hard, undercooked rice over the years. The wine most certainly helped things go down easier. The way everyone carried on discussing the children's teachers, who were locals that had also taught the Langdon trio, the new coffee shop that had replaced an old hardware store and one of their neighbors who was running for mayor, Dr. Grigsby wondered if she was the only one nearly dying from an abused palette.

This shit is awful! How come white people never season their damn food? This is something Yolanda would've said, and hearing Yolanda's voice as though she, too, were sitting at the table caused a chuckle to escape Dr. Grigsby.

"What's so funny?" Claude smiled at Dr. Grigsby as the table waited to be clued in on the joke. Before her giddy interruption, Ben was in the middle of telling everyone about a play he was involved in at school. Abashed, Dr. Grigsby cleared her throat, "I'm sorry, nothing. Will you excuse me? I need to use the restroom, please." She spoke quickly as she rose and slid her chair back while trying to ignore her sudden head rush at the same time.

Everyone looked puzzled, but Mrs. Langdon spoke up. "That's some good wine. Huh, dear?" She smiled and winked, sensing Dr. Grigsby's embarrassment. "Bathroom's at the end of the hall on the left."

Dr. Grigsby's heart drummed moderately but with much strength in her chest. She looked down at her hands as the warm water caused the soapy bubbles to slide from her palms and swirl down the drain into one of the dual sinks. They were shaking, and she didn't know why. *Everyone's so nice*, she thought. *What is wrong with me? It's that Davie. Something's up with that dude, man.* She could hear Christopher's menacing voice but it was in her head. She squeezed her eyes and popped them open, staring at herself in the mirror. "Get it together, Grigsby." She spoke aloud to her reflection but it was Jessica's voice that projected.

After taking ten slow deep breaths and drying her hands on the off-white embroidered hand towel, she opened the door and, startled, she leapt backwards grabbing her chest.

Davie stood on the other side. "Everything okay?"

Releasing the breath she held in, Dr. Grigsby answered, "You scared me".

"I'm sorry. I didn't mean to." Davie eyed her curiously before peering over her shoulder. "Is someone else in there with you? I thought I heard some voices."

"No. There's just me!" Dr. Grigsby tried to sound carefree and breezy. "It's all yours!"

When she rejoined the family in the dining room, Sarah and Mrs. Langdon had begun clearing the table. Dr. Grigsby was thankful she didn't have to swallow any more of the less than perfect meal. She was ready to redeem herself. "Can I help with anything?"

It was Sarah's turn to make her feel welcomed. "Sure, Helen. We're just getting ready for dessert. Why don't you grab the pie from the counter in the kitchen?" She spoke as she piled dishes on top of each other before carting them in her arms as she followed Dr. Grigsby to the kitchen. "I hope you like pumpkin pie. The knife's over there," she nodded with her head.

"Oh yeah, absolutely," Dr. Grigsby grinned. "These look great," she added as she lifted one pie in each hand. At Mrs. Langdon's instruction she set them in the center of the table then returned to the kitchen for the knife.

"Can you take these out too? I'm gonna load the dishwasher." Sarah pointed to a stack of small plates.

"Sure!" Dr. Grigsby began setting out the plates as Mrs. Langdon set out forks.

"This looks good, Mom." Claude beamed, glad to see his girlfriend getting along well with his family.

"It really does, honey." Mr. Langdon added. "I'm ready to dig in." He rubbed his stomach.

"Me too!"

"Me three!" Mandy and Ben agreed.

Davie returned to the dining room and leaned against the wall with his hand on his chin, his squinty expression reappearing. "Are you sure we haven't met before?"

Dr. Grigsby felt her insides flip flop. "I really don't think so."

"I swear you look so familiar." He insisted. Dr. Grigsby shrugged and gave a clueless smile.

"Davie, will you give it up. You don't have to know *every* woman in the state of New York." Claude teased.

"No, I'm serious. Have you ever been on TV or something? I know I've seen you somewhere before." He shook his head before taking a seat at the table. "It'll come to me."

Brian sat in silence and just looked on. He'd drank the most wine out of everyone and appeared ready for a bed. By the time everyone was seated again, Mrs. Langdon started to cut slices of pie to pass around the table. After the last piece made its way to Brian, she lay the knife against the edge of the remaining pie tin that sat in the center of the table.

"Can I have another slice?" Ben asked.

"Gosh you're so greedy, Ben." Mandy's disgust with her brother sprawled across her little round face.

"Am not!"

"Don't you two start," Sarah basted. "Ben, why don't you wait a few minutes? Let the first slice go down." Ben crossed his arms, leaned back and pouted.

"THE NEWS!" Brian suddenly blurted in a saucy bewilderment. "That's where you know her from, Davie. She's … that *guy*." He seemed confused by his own accusation.

"Guy? Brian, what are you talking about?" Claude laughed.

"Oh … my… god," the words dripped slowly from Davie's mouth, which now dropped open. "That's it! That's where I know you from. You were involved in all those robberies down by Albany and Troy. Your picture is posted all over the place. I *knew* I knew you!" Everyone's head turned right to left, their eyes darting here and there in bemusement.

Finally, "Brian, I think you and Davie have had enough wine for tonight, sweetie." Sarah was sure her husband was blabbering tipsy poppycock, but Davie's eyes never left Dr. Grigsby. He was studying her.

"He's right." He said, quietly. "You've done something different to your hair and, I must say you were very convincing dressed as a man, but we both know Brian's right. You're a criminal." At first the words fell out lightheartedly, almost a chuckle, like Davie was amused to have a celebrity of the sort amongst them. Then, as if the details of the robberies were being fed to him through a teleprompter, he recalled more. "You shot a guy! They've got you on video!" His amusement soon turned to alarm.

Dr. Grigsby sat stiff, unsure of herself. She knew what he was saying was nonsense. Yet, a different part of her felt like a wild animal that was backed into a corner. *Shit! Now what are we gonna do?* It was Christopher. *What do you mean, 'we'? I ain't have nothing to do with that.* Yolanda hissed. *You shot someone?* Somehow Jessica sounded almost innocent. The voices in her head were too many, too fast. "Will you all just be quiet?" Dr. Grigsby's face contorted and she grabbed the sides of her head as if she suffered from an excruciating migraine. She clutched onto one of the luxurious hair clips and tugged it out as she spoke. "I can't think straight if you're all going to talk at once!" The extension of fake black strands hit the edge of the table before floating to the floor.

Thinking she was speaking to the people in the room, Mrs. Langdon shushed everyone. "Everybody just quiet down now. Helen, is what they're saying true?"

Dr. Grigsby bit hard on her bottom lip, afraid and unsure of what may escape her lips next. She felt helpless. Her lack of control was such that some bigger, grander, puppet master was pulling her strings. Her eyes darted about all over the dining room in search of this invisible grand wizard so she could beg for mercy. There would be no mercy as the voices of Christopher, Yolanda and Jessica bickered on. Before she knew what was happening, her hand shot out and grasped the handle of the knife that sat on the table, its blade part shiny part crusty from dried on pie. "Everybody get back!" She jumped up, causing her chair to meet the floor with a hard bang, startling all.

"Helen, what do you think you're doing?" Claude stood and grabbed Dr. Grigsby's wrist. She swiftly twisted out of his grip and brought the knife down, slicing Claude's palm straight across. He looked in horror at the bright red drops quickly turned into streams, oozing from the straight line. The pain hadn't registered through the shock yet.

Sarah gasped. "Mandy. Ben, come here, honey." The kids quickly ran into their mother's arms as she crowded them to one corner of the room. Mandy began to whimper. The men stood slowly, leaving only Mrs. Langdon seated at the table, her face a mixture of worry and sympathy. Mr. Langdon stood behind her with his hands on her shoulders. No one dared to make a sudden move.

"What are you doing? You – you cut me!" Claude used the bottom of his plaid button-up shirt to compress the bleeding. It quickly saturated as the blood ran through the thin material and droplets splattered onto the marble floor.

Dr. Grigsby's hand shook noticeably as she held the knife pointed in Claude's direction. "I-I – I'm sorry." The words sounded as if she was unsure if she should be apologetic or not.

"Honey, why don't you just put the knife down and we can all talk about whatever's bothering you?" Mrs. Langdon's calmness appealed to Dr. Grigsby's sense of judgement, but

Davie's counteracted any parts of her that might've been willing to recede.

"This is crazy! Just put the damn knife down! Can't you see he's hurt? He needs medical attention. I'm calling the police!" Davie turned towards the dining room entry, but Dr. Grigsby sprinted from her side of the table to meet him at the doorway, bumping her hip into the corner of the table as she went. The table rocked and Brian's glass of wine swished back and forth, threatening to leap onto the white table cloth.

"You! You couldn't just leave it alone. Could you?" Dr. Grigsby held the tip of the blade just inches from Davie's abdomen, but it was Christopher's voice that growled, lowly, from the pit of her stomach. "One more step and I'll gut you right here."

"Helen! For god's sake!" Claude pleaded, still clutching his injured hand.

"Mommy, I'm scared." Mandy whimpered with tears streaming down her chubby tomato cheeks.

Dr. Grigsby turned towards the sound, the knife still in the air at arm's length. "You don't need to be scared." She slowly put one foot in front of the other, careful not to take her attention off of Davie, as she crept towards the corner where Sarah clung to her cubs. "I wouldn't hurt you. Mommy loves you." Again, Dr. Grigsby's lips moved, but now it was Bhavna's turn to speak. She slowly lowered her arm, letting the knife dangle near her thigh. "It's okay. Come to Mommy. I'll keep you safe." Mandy only stared back in response. "Zobia, it's okay. No need to be afraid. See?" A crazed smile spread across Dr. Grigsby's face. "Nirav, you're not afraid. Are you, my little man?" She spoke to Ben. Her free hand reached out, inviting the children towards her, but no one moved.

"Don't you dare come near my kids," Sarah's voice was stern and even.

"Ooh oh, Dr. Grigsby, I don't know about this. The kids. You said I shouldn't be around the kids. Remember? Ooh no, no, no. This is bad. I shouldn't be here, Dr. Grigsby. Why are we here?" Dr. Grigsby's pulse quickened, filled with Jessica's increasing nervousness.

"Shut up, baby killer!" Christopher warned.

"Yo, Chris, you need to calm down. I can't get mixed up in anymore bullshit. I can't go back to jail. I'm already on probation." Yolanda warned.

"My name is Christopher, to you, not Chris."

"Okay, well, Christ-o-ferr. You trippin' and you need to put that knife down, dude." Yolanda warned.

The family looked on at this one woman show as Dr. Grigsby's voice and demeanor changed with every other sentence that left her mouth. Claude continued to plead and try to reason with his love, but Dr. Grigsby's patients were out of control and his voice was just background noise now amongst the chaos. The defiant group of misfits never heard Brian creep up from behind Dr. Grigsby. He grabbed her, but she was a lot stronger than she looked. He managed to get only part of her into a bear hug, leaving the hand that clung to the knife free to thrash about wildly through the air. Mr. Langdon misjudged his own ability as he leapt from his stance behind Mrs. Langdon to try to take hold of the knife-wielding arm. He missed and caught air instead.

"I said stay back!" It was Christopher's voice but Dr. Grigsby's hand that plunged the knife between Mr. Langdon's ribs. It wasn't until she jerked the knife back out that they all realized how deep the wound was. Brian immediately let go, sending Dr. Grigsby stumbling forward, slicing the air with the blade. Blood flew onto the wall. Mr. Langdon pressed into his side. No words formed, only a groan before he, too, stumbled onto the floor, grabbing the table cloth on his way down.

"Jack!" Mrs. Langdon tumbled out of her chair clumsily, landing on her knees by her husband's side. She cradled his head with one arm. The other arm wandered aimlessly, hovering over his body as she frantically searched for the perfect place to rest her hand. There was so much blood pouring out she didn't know what to do.

Christopher turned his attention back to Davie. "I knew something was up with you. I knew you couldn't be trusted."

Dr. Grigsby spoke as she jabbed and cut the air in front of Davie. He jumped back, dodging from one side to the other.

"Please," was all he managed to eek out, careful not to further agitate Dr. Grigsby. Dr. Grigsby tilted her head back and cackled in response. Her eye's – Christopher's eyes bulged crazily like they would pop right out of the sockets. Suddenly she felt Brian's burly bodyweight thrusted against her own, his arms wrapped tightly pinning her arms to her sides. They went down together with a thud, and Dr. Grigsby's head slammed into the hard floor face first. Everything went black. No more voices were heard, inside her head or otherwise. Just nothing.

7 HELEN GRIGSBY

"And how long have you been treating Ms. Grigsby?"

"Six years," Dr. Planthers sounded exhausted.

"Who is her next of kin?"

"She has a brother in Florida, but I haven't been able to reach him. They haven't been on speaking terms for some time now. Ever since…" Her voice trailed. She wrung her hands as she debated whether she should share the information or not. She already felt somewhat responsible for Helen's being here, half unconscious and cuffed to the bedrail at the hospital. She didn't want to violate their confidentiality.

The room felt tight with four people in there, the hospital bed taking up most of the square footage. The privacy curtain was partially pulled around the bed, shrinking the space even more. Hospital staff bustled back and forth outside of the cracked door. Inside the room, the monitor stood, hooked up to Helen, in the corner. A chair sat stationed in another corner on the opposite side of the bed. There was a TV mounted high up on the wall. The news showed, but someone muted the volume. There was a bathroom at the back of the room and a small window was just outside of it. Dr. Planthers looked towards it as if the answers were somewhere out there.

"Since?" The officer asked while the attending physician, Dr. Chin, took his own notes nearby. The three convened at the foot of the bed.

Dr. Planthers glanced nervously at Helen, who lay still with only the machines next to her beeping and pinging to show signs of life. Her head was bandaged. "There was an … incident."

"Incident?" The officer questioned. Dr. Chin paused with his pen positioned on his clipboard, ready to resume. He peered over the rims of his spectacles as he waited for Dr. Planthers to explain.

"Yeah…with her niece." Dr. Planthers felt guilty for betraying her client, but she knew it was time. She could no longer help her. "Helen was visiting her brother and his family a while back – this was before I started treating her. She offered to babysit for her brother and sister-in-law while they went out for a date night. The niece must've been around two years old back then. Helen's brother came home to find her giving the child a bath. Only…"

"Only what?" The officer pressed.

"She – Helen was holding the little girl under the water." It was obvious that Dr. Planthers was uneasy retelling the story as though she'd witnessed the event herself. She recalled when Helen first told her the story, how detached she seemed while telling it. Dr. Planthers kept a cool exterior for the sake of professionalism but she was horrified on the inside. She imagined the child's skin soft and rosy from the warm water. Her chubby legs, as children of that age often carry baby fat, thrashing about, wildly, splashing water onto the walls and floor as she fought for her life. She pictured Helen holding her down with both hands firmly around her tiny neck, maybe a crazed look on her face. Dr. Planthers shuddered at the reenactment taking place in her mind.

"You're saying she tried to drown the child?" Dr. Chin was in disbelief.

Dr. Planthers nodded. "If her brother hadn't arrived at that exact moment there's no telling what would've happened." The trio shared a brief instant of uncomfortable silence. "He went ballistic, understandably, when he found them. He didn't understand. He *couldn't* understand. He probably didn't even realize that Helen wasn't herself. She needed help."

"What do you mean she wasn't herself?" The officer didn't follow. As far as he could see, so far, before them lay a woman who'd sliced up her boyfriend and tried to murder his father. Now he learned that she'd tried to kill before. And an innocent child? Like Helen's brother, he couldn't understand either. She didn't need help. She needed the electric chair.

"It was Jessica acting out."

"Jessica?" Both Dr. Chin and the officer asked in unison.

Dr. Planthers released a weary sigh. "Helen suffers from a multiple personality disorder – or Dissociative Identity Disorder as some are calling it these days and Borderline Schizophrenia."

"Oh, so she's gonna try to use the nuttier than a fruitcake defense." The officer wasn't buying it.

"Dissociative identity and schizophrenia are serious conditions, officer. A person suffering from either one, independently, can become really dangerous. Nevermind someone who suffers from both." Dr. Chin weighed in.

Dr. Planthers nodded in agreement before continuing, "Since treating Helen, I've been able to identify at least four separate identities; not including herself of course. One male and three females, and, until recently, I don't even think each one was aware of the other. There could be others that just haven't surfaced yet. It's hard to say how many there are for sure. The uncommon thing is that she looks at each of these personalities as her patients. She, herself, is suffering from these mental disorders, but each one of them is also suffering from some other sort of disorder. She's appointed herself as their psychologist, going as far as referring to herself as 'doctor'." Dr. Planthers continued aloud, but her next comment was more to herself, "Could have something to do with her psychology studies in college."

"She studied psychology?" Dr. Chin was just as dumbfounded as Dr. Planthers had been at her onset of treating Dr. Grigsby.

"Yes, NYU actually, and she did quite well. She probably would've continued to excel in med school had she not experienced that awful loss, her parents' death. They died in a bad car accident during her residency. That's when she had her first psychotic break."

"Who is Ashok?" Dr. Chin questioned. "At one point she was kind of mindlessly moaning the name Ashok a few times. Is he one of the personalities?"

"No. I believe Ashok is one of her lovers. She has many. Even been picked up for soliciting." Dr. Planthers' voice was dismal. "But as you know, Dr. Chin, patients like these often build entire fantasy worlds around just the thinnest sliver of fact."

"Mmhmm," Dr. Chin clasped his chin with his pen cradled between his fingers.

"One of her identities she calls Bhavna. In her fantasy world Ashok is Bhavna's husband and they have two small children together. Ashok is indeed real, and they've been involved on and off for a very long time; since before I even started treating her. I suspect Ashok may actually be married to someone else, but he just humors Helen on the side. Leave it to her, though, and he rescued her from a life of poverty in Assam. I'm fairly certain Helen has never even set foot in India, but these are the types of fabricated stories she lives out in her mind. Bhavna is also some type of talented violinist. Helen did play violin for a period during her adolescence."

"That would be another sliver of fact." The officer honed in, trying to make sense of it all.

"Right. Bhavna even has a lover on the side who is the conductor of the fictitious orchestra she belongs to. I forget his name. Steve or Stanley, I think." Dr. Planthers' forehead wrinkled as she tried to recall Stephen's name. "Whatever. I honestly think he's just another random man she casually met somewhere, but in her mind – Bhavna's mind, he is her sophisticated paramour."

"Wow!" This was all over the officer's head and out of the norm of his line of work. Sure, he'd locked up a crazy here and there for public disturbances, but he never had any in depth knowledge of what was wrong with them. He usually just chalked it all up to drug use.

"Bhavna is the driving force behind Helen's promiscuity. She's the nymphomaniac of the group."

"A sex addict." The officer confirmed.

"Yes."

"Well, who's responsible for the bank robberies? That's who we're most interested in. I mean I know Ms. Grigsby is who we've been looking for. She matches the sketches and we picked up one of her crew members. He gave her right up. Didn't take much coaxing once a deal was on the table. We didn't believe him at first when he insisted the ring leader was a woman. You don't usually see that type of thing, but I did some digging and I do see that she has quite the rap sheet. If I'm not mistaken, I think I even saw something about arson from her younger years." Dr. Planthers nodded in confirmation. She knew that was probably Yolanda's work. "So, I guess what I'm asking is which *personality* is the robber, Dr. Planthers?" A twinge of annoyance shot through Dr. Planthers at the officer's use of air quotes when he said "personality".

"That would be Christopher, one of the most dangerous." Dr. Planthers dropped her eyes to the tiled floor. There was a black scuff mark near the officer's foot. "I still can't believe things have gotten this bad for her. She must've needed the money. She's been living off of disability but it's barely enough to get by, and she can't hold a steady job. Christopher is the only one that scares even me, and I suspect that's who stabbed that poor man."

"Mr. Langdon you mean?" The officer asked.

"Yes."

"What's Ms. Grigsby's relation to the Langdon's anyway? What was she doing at their home?" He asked.

"She and Mr. Langdon's son, Claude Langdon, are something of an item. And I blame myself for that." Dr. Planthers exhaled heavily and shook her head. "Every year we – a group of my colleagues and I host an event where our patients can come and feel safe socializing with each other. Their conditions can sometimes alienate them from their peers. They met at our auction."

"I see." The officer jotted something on his notepad.

"Claude happens to be a patient of mine as well."

"What's his deal?"

"I won't disclose that to you. I've already jeopardized my practice by telling you about Helen. Claude is harmless. He's a sweet man. I remember how much he gushed over Helen in our meetings. I didn't think it was a good idea. I knew he couldn't possibly know the depths of Helen's issues. I tried to discourage it, but they were determined to be together and it's not like they were breaking the law or anything. So, my hands were pretty much tied." Dr. Planthers' bottom lip quivered, and she almost looked like she would break down and cry, but she didn't. "He's the one who called me today. He sounded so awful on the phone. I really should see him. Who knows what kind of effect this will have on his progress. He's come such a long way."

"We'll need official reports from both of you and, Dr. Planthers, I think it might be a good idea for you to join us once she's well enough to begin interrogation," the officer instructed. Both Dr. Chin and Dr. Planthers nodded in response.

***

Dr. Planthers found Claude pacing back and forth near the nurses' station of Intensive Care as soon as she stepped out of the elevator. The blood on his shirt had turned brown. It wasn't like him to have such a disheveled appearance with the right side of his shirt hanging out of his pants and the other side tucked in. One hand hung by his side bandaged in a wad of white gauze. The other rested atop of his head. After packing the wound with antibiotics and sealing it with twelve stiches, the emergency room doctor still had a difficult time getting his blood to clot so that the bleeding would stop. Because of the amount of blood loss, they wanted to keep him under observation a little longer but, after much persistence, Claude convinced them to release him to be with his family while they waited for news of Mr. Langdon's condition. "You come right back downstairs if you bleed through this gauze." The doctor had sternly instructed against his better judgement.

Dr. Planthers rushed towards Claude with open arms, "Oh Claude." She came to a quick halt, almost tripping over her own feet when she suddenly remembered Claude's discomfort with being touched. Instead of the hug her instincts initially led her to give, she gave only a light pat on the shoulder. "I got here as soon as I could."

"Thank you, Dr. Planthers. How is she?" Claude's face was that of a lost child.

"She's still not awake, but the attending physician seems to think she'll recover from the blow."

"I just don't understand any of this. One moment she was fine. The next moment she ..." Claude furrowed his brow and scanned the floor in search of words. "It was like it was her body but someone else was inside. Even her voice was different."

Dr. Planthers' eyes were filled with empathy for the love-struck man. "How are *you*, Claude?"

Back to rubbing his head, he answered, "I-I don't even know. Still in shock I guess."

"What are they saying about your father?"

"It's still touch and go. She punctured a lung when she...she...," his voice quivered as a knot formed and he fought back tears. He couldn't bring himself to say what his girlfriend had done. He cleared his throat, "One of his lungs filled with a lot of blood before collapsing. They've been working on him, but he's not out of the woods yet." Dr. Planthers grimaced. "I just don't understand how she could do such a thing. I just don't know what possessed her, Dr. Planthers. That's what it was like – like she was possessed by the devil himself!"

"Claude, Helen isn't well and she hasn't been for a while. There's a lot you don't know about her."

"Yeah, apparently!" he scoffed.

***

"Oh my god, I'm so bored!" Jessica complained two days later as Dr. Grigsby still lay in the same position.

"You complain too much," Bhavna was tired of waiting too.

"I wish all of y'all would just shut the hell up, honestly," Yolanda was irritated. She had things to do, and now she was stuck. They were all stuck.

"Yeah, really," Christopher agreed.

"You're the reason we're all trapped here! I told you to be easy but nooooooo! You had to go and stick the poor old bastard. Now look at us!" Yolanda wasn't about to let Christopher forget so soon where his actions had led them.

"It was an accident. I didn't mean to hurt him." He said the words but his demeanor didn't hold nearly an ounce of remorse.

"But you did. You are a selfish man, only concerned with yourself." Bhavna's accent came out choppy.

Christopher smirked. "That's not what you said at the grocery store."

The group could hear the heart monitor speed up as Bhavna was overcome with shame, causing Helen's pulse to quicken.

"Shhh shhh," Yolanda hushed the other voices. "Somebody's coming in."

The heart rate increase prompted a nurse to come in to check on Helen. Dr. Chin followed soon after. He entered just as the nurse held Helen's wrist while looking at a watch. "Is she awake?" Dr. Chin asked as he joined the nurse at the bedside.

"No, still not awake. Every so often the monitor spikes. I can't figure out why, though."

Dr. Chin sighed. "Well, if all of her levels look okay, don't worry about it too much. Just keep watch."

"Poor thing," the nurse didn't know the whole back story as to how her patient wound up under her care.

"This poor thing's going to jail for a long time." Dr. Chin disclosed.

"For real?"

"For real. She stabbed a man, and I just heard back from downstairs that he didn't make it. Our patient here is facing homicidal charges. We have to keep a close eye, make sure she doesn't try anything."

"How could she try anything? She's barely even conscious." The nurse said.

"Still, you never know what a person is capable of."

ABOUT THE AUTHOR

Just Jewel is an author, poet and blogger from New Jersey. She holds an Associate's Degree in Business Administration and a Bachelor's Degree in Creative Writing and English (with a concentration in fiction). Her work has appeared in publications such as RnB Magazine, Black Girl Seeks and A Drop of Jewel blog site. The author resides in Texas where she divides her time between work in the insurance industry, writing and entrepreneurship.

<u>Titles By Just Jewel</u>

Dr. Grigsby's Clients

God Bless the Church Folk

The Mini Poetry Project Vol. I: A Collection of Random Expressions

Two Way Mirrors